Fighting BACK

Book 6 of The Ravaged Land Series.

By
Kellee L. Greene

This is a work of fiction. Names, characters, organizations, places, events and incidents are either products of the author's imagination or are used fictitiously. Any resemblance to actual persons, living or dead, events or locales is entirely coincidental.

Copyright © 2017 Kellee L. Greene

First Edition July 2017

Books By Kellee L. Greene

Ravaged Land Series

Ravaged Land -Book 1
Finding Home - Book 2
Crashing Down - Book 3
Running Away - Book 4
Escaping Fear - Book 5
Fighting Back - Book 6

The Alien Invasion Series

The Landing - Book 1
The Aftermath - Book 2

Destined Realms Series

Destined - Book 1

For My Readers
THANK YOU!

Chapter one.

There were times I was sure that when the sun came up, I wouldn't wake to meet the new day. Eventually, my time would run out, but somehow, I was still alive. I wasn't sure how I'd made it as long as I had, but for once, I was glad that I had.

We still constantly worried that HOME would find us. If they did, we wanted to be ready for them.

Things had been going exceptionally well for Penn, Carter and me. Our basement was packed with supplies, the fence around our property was coming along nicely, and we had a large amount of food and water stored up that would easily last us the winter, if not longer.

With each passing day, Penn grew more and more confident that Nora hadn't had time to reveal our location or much of anything at all to HOME. If she had, they likely would have come for us. It was very likely that she just hadn't gotten the chance to alert them under the circumstances.

It was my fault that she had gotten as close to us as she had. I should have been more suspicious of her, even back when I first met her at HOME's brainwashing facility. I should have known better. I shouldn't have ever brought her back to our place.

I had been under such stress - deprived of adequate food, water, and sleep - that I hadn't been thinking straight. The pain from the broken or bruised rib had been overwhelming, not to mention my need to get back to my safe place with Penn and Carter.

I would have done anything to get back to them. In fact, I had.

My mind had been so focused on getting back that I gave her the benefit of the doubt. Which it turned out, she didn't deserve.

Thankfully, that was all over now, even though it often played back in my mind. I really should have known better. Should have done better.

We had so many supplies gathered up that it would have been very hard to leave. It would have taken us forever to start over again, even if we could manage trekking out there and locating a new place.

Winter was here, and the snow was falling. If we had to go out into the world, I was sure we wouldn't survive in the cold and snow. Starting over just didn't seem like an option.

So, together, we decided to stay and fight, if it came to that. Of course, we hoped HOME wouldn't come, but if they did, we'd protect what we had no matter what the cost. Even if that cost was our lives.

I was sick of running. If they came, we'd stand our ground and defend what we'd built, but we all hoped it wouldn't come to that. Hopefully, HOME would just stay far away. It wasn't like we wanted revenge or any kind of contact with HOME whatsoever.

HOME could have their part of the world, and we'd have ours. All we wanted was to stay hidden and live out the rest of our lives in peace. No more struggling. No more loss.

"I still wish we had more," Penn said as he stomped up the basement stairs.

"You say that every time you come upstairs," I said wrapping the blanket tighter around my shoulders. Every day it was getting colder and colder outside, which meant it was also a little colder inside.

"We don't know how long the winter will last. What if it's as extreme as the first big one?" Penn asked as he poured himself a cup of water.

I shook my head. I couldn't even guess what this winter would be like, but we'd done everything we could to prepare.

"We'll freeze to death in this horribly insulated place if it gets as cold as it did in Alaska after the big storm," Penn said. His eyes shifted over to the collection of boots and winter jackets he'd gathered on his last run.

The boots he'd found for me were a little too big, and the jacket had a small hole in the arm, but I hoped I wouldn't need to use them for much other than a quick run outside. We had plenty of blankets. We had a fireplace. As long as it was a typical winter and not a freakishly cold winter, we'd be fine.

There was a knock at the front door, but it was a knock I recognized. It was the secret knock we always used.

I popped up and peeked out of the window before opening the door even though I knew who was on the other side. The cold winter air blew into the house and caused me to shiver.

"Ugh!" Carter said stepping inside and closing the door behind himself. He flipped the locks into place and stomped the snow off of his large, fur-lined boots. "So… freaking… cold… out… there."

Penn glanced at me and then raised his eyebrows. The air hadn't felt any different from any other day as far as I could tell.

"Like abnormally cold?" Penn asked.

"Not sure. This will be my first Michigan winter, so I don't know what to expect. But I don't think so. It just feels cold," Carter said as he placed a couple of snowflake-covered logs next to the fireplace.

Even though it seemed like a lifetime ago, we'd all been through the same long, crazy-cold winter, although it hadn't been together. I had been warm in the shelter waiting it out, but Penn had been in Alaska suffering through the cold with only a fire to keep him warm inside his father's house.

Sometime I'd have to ask Carter about his life before he'd met us. I didn't know how he'd survived the winter but he never really seemed to want to talk about his past. I was pretty sure it was too painful. It was something that reminded him too much of his sister, and it wasn't that long ago he'd lost her to the sickness.

"Did you see anyone while you were out there? Anything I need to know about?" Penn asked rubbing his thumb hard against his index finger. It was like he was ready to pull a trigger on his invisible gun. I was pretty sure I could hear his teeth grinding together as he waited for Carter's answer.

"Are you serious? Don't you think if I saw someone you'd be the first to know? It would be the first thing I said when I walked through the door. Trust me," Carter said kicking off his boots as he turned to check the lock on the door… again. "Do you really think they'll still come? It's been several weeks now and nothing."

"No. Probably not. I mean, I don't know. They could have some kind of plan, or come here unrelated to what happened with Nora." Penn walked over and started pacing in front of the crackling fire.

"They are going to do the 'let's wait until they least expect it' attack plan," I muttered.

"I have no idea what they will or won't do. You guys have way more experience with HOME than I do," Carter said kneeling on the floor next to the fireplace. He put his hands so close I thought they'd catch fire.

I stepped in front of Penn to stop his pacing and looked up into his eyes. "For whatever it's worth, I don't think they are coming. At least not because of something Nora did," I said with a shrug. "But they *will* come. Hopefully a long time from now."

Penn nodded and looked down at my fingers. He grabbed my hand and wrapped his warm hands around mine.

It looked like he was going to say something, probably more about HOME, but then he stopped himself. His expression changed.

"Your fingers are so cold," Penn said.

"Yeah." I looked down at his warm hands holding mine. "They've been like that ever since my fight to get back here to you and Carter. I just can't seem to get them to warm up."

Penn looked at me with concern filling his gorgeous eyes. "Can you feel them? They move alright?"

"Yeah, they're fine for the most part," I said with a smile. "They just get cold really easily."

At first he looked at me as though he wasn't sure if I was telling the truth, but then a half-smile appeared on his face. "Well, I can try to keep them warm for you," he said, leaning towards me slightly, my cheeks warming when he didn't let go of my hand.

Carter cleared his throat as though he thought he was interrupting something. I was tempted to pull my hand away, but truthfully, Penn's warm skin felt nice.

"So, what are we going to do all winter locked up in this place?" Carter asked.

"I'll tell you what we *are* going to do... we are going to not worry about all the things we have to do," I said with a weak laugh. That's all I wanted, but somehow I doubted that's what I'd get.

They'd be off trekking through a foot of snow trying to gather more supplies. But what I wanted them to do, was to relax and take it easy for a while. The whole point of finding this place was so that we could stop.

"I have an idea," Penn said wearing a mischievous grin.

"Oh, boy," I said cocking my head to the side as I waited to hear his plan.

Carter stepped closer as if he was

ready to get started on whatever Penn was about to suggest even without knowing what it was. "I'm all ears," Carter said rubbing his palms together.

"OK. We build… wow, this is probably going to sound totally crazy, but since the basement floor is dirt we could make an underground hideout. Maybe a tunnel in case we need to make a quick escape," Penn said as he looked back and forth between Carter and me. He was squinting slightly as though he was afraid our reaction would sting. It looked like he was expecting us both to shoot down his idea.

"Won't the ground be frozen?" I asked.

Penn shook his head. "Should work that far under. Frostline won't be that deep."

"We have shovels," Carter said stroking his chin with his thumb and index finger. I couldn't tell if he was considering the idea or anxious to get started on the tunnel project immediately. "It'd take awhile to complete such a task."

"We have nothing but time," Penn said.

They both turned to me as if they

wanted my approval… as if I was the deciding factor. I twisted a few strands of hair between my fingers and tugged slightly.

"If you think it's a good idea then I'm all for it, but I'm not sure how much digging I'm willing to contribute to this project," I said rubbing my side.

My rib was better from when it had been broken, bruised or whatever, but I was terrified of injuring it again. I remembered the pain like it happened yesterday and I still had no idea how I survived it. If it happened again, I didn't think I could bear it, and I was in the comfort of our own home.

Penn nodded. I was fairly certain he understood since he had been the one to hold my hand when I couldn't sleep at night because the pain was too much. He had been the one to help me get well again, but I could still feel a soreness that I wasn't sure would ever go away. I wondered if it hadn't healed properly.

I was careful with all my movements, afraid that a sudden turn would make the pain come back.

"We aren't in a hurry to get anything done, but who knows, maybe someday it could save our lives," Penn said clapping his hands together once as if that settled it.

When there was another clapping noise, we all looked at Penn's hands, but this time the sound hadn't come from him. The sound had come from somewhere outside, and it was a noise we all recognized.

I looked at Penn, and he pulled me into the bedroom. He guided me to the corner of the room furthest from the window and put his hands against the wall on each side of me. Penn took a step closer and pinned me into the corner.

He looked at me and then down at the space between us. It looked as though he was trying to hear something.

When there was another gunshot in the distance, he squeezed my arms and lowered himself so he was looking directly into my eyes. The switch had flipped, and he wasn't regular Penn anymore, he was Penn that had been trained by HOME.

"Wait here," he said.

"Penn, I can help," I said, but he clenched his teeth and pointed at the ground. Ever since I'd been hurt, he'd been extra worried about me like I was an extremely delicate porcelain doll... but I wasn't a doll. Far from it. For the most part, excluding my rib, I felt like I was the opposite. "Come

14

on!"

"Just wait!" he said before he dashed to the window.

The gunshots rang out, one after the other, but I couldn't tell how close they were to our place. Carter appeared in the bedroom doorway with his winter boots and hat on. He was holding his gun, ready to do whatever was asked of him.

"Are we going or what?" Carter asked.

Penn held up his index finger and pressed it against his lips. He wanted absolute silence while he focused on what was going on.

Then, there was another shot. I didn't need to have Penn's abilities to know that it had gotten closer. Much too close.

Chapter two.

    Carter stood there tapping his foot waiting for Penn to give the word. He put all his faith in the fact that Penn would know what to do. Penn had yet to lead us astray. One thing was for sure, Penn would always know better than I would how to handle pretty much any situation.

    After a few more gunshots rang out, we started to hear the howls. One right after the other.

    Penn looked at me and then at Carter. His expression was blank as he turned back to peek out between the curtains.

    "They're killing dog-beasts," Penn whispered so quietly I wasn't sure I'd heard him correctly. But with each whiny howl, I knew that I had. His assessment sounded horrifyingly accurate.

    "Do you think it's HOME?" I asked, my voice softer than a whisper.

    He shook his head side to side as

though he wasn't sure one way or the other who was responsible. How could he be? It might have been anyone out there, we definitely couldn't rule out the possibility that it was HOME. After all, no one liked the dog-beasts, at least that's how it seemed.

After a few more minutes, the cries and gunshots lessened. They sounded as though they were getting further and further away from the house, until we couldn't hear them at all. Whatever had been going on out there was over.

We stood there in silence for at least ten more minutes, if not longer, after we'd heard the last gunshot. It seemed as though they were gone, but I figured Penn wanted to be absolutely certain.

Someone, or a group of someone's, had passed through the area, thankfully not close enough to the house to know we were here. Of course, that didn't mean they wouldn't be back. Even if they hadn't found us this time, there was always a chance they'd find us the next time.

"We start the tunnel. Now. Let's get the shovels," Penn said and followed Carter out of the bedroom.

"Can I move now?" I said sarcastically as I held as still as a mannequin. If Penn picked up on my tone, he ignored it.

"Yes, but stay inside. Lock the door behind us. We'll be right back," Penn said, and then I heard the front door close.

I crossed my arms and leaned back against the wall as I rolled my eyes. He wouldn't ever see me as anything but fragile.

"Ugh," I said letting out a breath as I pushed myself away from the wall to go lock the door and wait patiently for them to come back.

I knew they wouldn't be gone for long, but if I didn't lock the door, I'd probably have to listen to a twenty-minute lecture about why it's always better to lock the door than it is to leave it open. It was a speech I'd heard before. I was almost surprised Penn hadn't written it out and pinned it to the wall next to the door.

I kept peeking out between the curtains waiting for them to walk into view. It felt like it was taking them far longer than it should have just to grab the shovels and come back.

I looked down at my feet trying to see if I could hear them moving around outside. It hadn't been more than a second or two before I heard the secret knock. My whole body jolted even though I had been expecting them. Apparently, I was a little jumpy.

I peeked out of the curtains to verify that it was, in fact, them and that no one was hiding out in the distance. When I saw only Penn and Carter, I opened the door.

"Damn, it's cold out there," Carter said loudly as he rubbed his upper arms. He set down his gun and locked the door once Penn was inside.

"Well you could have worn your jacket," I said shaking my head at them.

"It was just to the garage and back," Carter said.

I crossed my arms and stared at him. I wasn't sure how cold it was out there, but I was sure it was cold enough that they both should have taken their jackets, even for the short time they'd been gone.

"What if something would have happened, or if you would have gotten locked out there?" I said, but they both ignored me. "You were out there for like fifteen minutes. Maybe you have frostbite or something."

"We were not," Penn said as he walked towards the basement carrying one of the shovels. Carter had the other.

"Sure felt like it to me," I mumbled, but their feet were already pounding against the old wooden stairs.

I double checked the lock before sitting down on the sofa. I could hear their muffled voices through the floor, but I couldn't make out what they were saying. If I had to guess, Penn was probably telling Carter exactly what they were going to do, and Carter was probably standing there with his hands on his hips nodding enthusiastically.

After a short while, the stairs started creaking. Someone was coming up already, maybe Penn's idea wasn't going to work. I quickly grabbed a book off of the end-table and pretended to read.

Penn turned the corner, and I saw him glance in my direction before stepping into the kitchen to pour himself a cup of water. We had jugs and bottles of water stored in the basement and a small supply that we kept upstairs.

In the winter it was easy to replenish our water supplies since all we had to do was gather, melt and boil the snow. It was much easier than walking out to the frozen-over lake through the deep snow.

The lake area seemed pretty dangerous. It was hard to get to the water with all the snow and ice that built up along the shoreline and over the pier. Even though the snow around the water looked thick enough, we were pretty sure it was far too dangerous to walk on. If anyone ever fell through into the frigid water below it would probably kill them. So, thankfully, because of all the snow around the house, we didn't have to venture out to the lake.

"How's it going down there?" I said without taking my eyes off the book.

"Fine. Think it's going to work out, but we can't both dig at the same time," Penn said before taking a long drink. "Not enough room. We'll have to take turns."

"Isn't it too dark down there?"

"We have the lanterns set up," Penn said and set his cup down roughly on the counter near the sink. "We can even work at night if we want to."

"Sounds like a good time."

Digging the tunnel would keep both Penn and Carter busy. They both probably liked the idea of having something to do and something that could save our lives if HOME ever came our way.

Penn walked over and sat down next

to me. He leaned forward with his elbows on his knees. After a few minutes, he stretched his arms over his head and leaned back, resting his arm on top of the cushion behind me.

"Is that any good?" he asked, and it took me a few moments to realize he was talking about the book in my hands. I had no idea if the book was good or not since I had read the same sentence at least thirty-seven times.

"Yeah, I guess," I said with a smile. I set the book down on my knee and looked over at him. "How long do you think that's going to take?"

"The tunnel?"

I nodded.

"Hmm... I'm not sure." Penn shook his head. "We'll dig the secret hiding slash supply area first, and then the escape tunnel. I have no idea where that will go exactly, or how I'll disguise the exit, but I have time to figure that out."

His leg was bouncing up and down as if he was nervous or anxious. More than his usual amount.

"Everything OK?" I asked tilting my head slightly.

"Yeah. I think it's going to work out,

it's just going to take time," Penn said looking at me with a half-smile. I wasn't sure if he was entirely convinced that it would work, but either way, it was worth a shot. A backup plan was better than no backup plan at all. "It'll give Carter and me something to do other than sitting around waiting for HOME to come knocking."

I'd still sit around waiting for HOME, but I didn't need to tell Penn that. After all, I'd spent almost all my time after knowing HOME existed waiting for them to come for me. It wasn't anything new. If I told Penn that, it would just make his knee bounce faster than it already was.

"You think they'll knock?" I said grinning at him.

"Probably not."

"Didn't think so."

"I'll do what I can to keep us safe... you don't have to worry," he said patting my shoulder before he pushed himself off of the sofa.

He walked into the bedroom, and I could hear the bedsprings squeak as he lowered himself onto the bed. It wouldn't surprise me if he slept until Carter was done and then go dig all night long.

Once he put his mind to something,

he'd see it through. Penn and Carter would finish that tunnel, no matter how long it took.

I wanted to ask where all the dirt was going to go, but they probably had it all figured out. It wouldn't be long before they'd start hauling buckets and buckets of dirt through the front door.

If Penn's tunnel idea worked, and HOME came, we could escape, but for how long? Where would we go?

We'd have to run again. We wouldn't be able to avoid HOME forever. Eventually, they'd catch up to us.

Chapter three.

Roughly two months had passed since Penn and Carter started the tunnel. No one had come around, and the snow continued to accumulate.

The snow was thick and wet. Even when the sun would pop out and melt some of it, more would fall soon, replacing and adding to what was already out there.

The progress Penn and Carter had made on the tunnel was amazing. They had worked hard, and I didn't think either of them had taken a day off since they started.

When Penn brought me down to show me what they'd accomplished, I couldn't even find the entrance. He smiled, and I realized that was exactly what he'd planned. Penn hadn't wanted the way in to be easily detected.

"There," he said pointing to the back of the room.

There was a shelving unit placed over a slab of wood that covered the entrance. It was completely undetectable unless you knew exactly where to look.

"Lucky we found a house with a dirt floor basement," I said as Penn moved the shelving unit out of the way.

"Who knows, maybe we could have found a jackhammer on one of our runs," Penn said with a straight face, but I was pretty sure he was joking.

He tipped up the board, so I was looking down the hole they'd dug. They'd taken pieces of wood and secured them to the wall with dirt. The steps didn't shift in the slightest as I climbed down.

At the bottom of the makeshift ladder was a small room which already was storing a few supplies. They'd brought down some bottles of water and several packages of snack bars which would stay there in case of an emergency. If HOME ever came and we had to hide, we could be stuck in the hideout for days.

"Should bring down more food," I said. My mind stuck on the idea of being trapped down in the small area.

"Yeah, of course," Penn said with his hands on his hips watching me as I checked out their work. "Probably a couple blankets too."

I could see where they had started digging the tunnel that would lead away from the house. What they'd done in such a short amount of time was simply amazing.

"This is really great!" I said lightly dragging my fingertips against the walls, feeling the little grains of dirt. The air was damp and smelled like fresh rain mixed with sweaty socks.

Penn and Carter both smiled. I could tell that they were both proud of their work.

"Thanks," Penn said wrapping his arm around my shoulders.

"Now you guys can take a break," I said, but I knew they wouldn't stop until the tunnel was finished.

In the months that had passed since they'd started digging, it had been quiet. Peaceful even. Nothing had happened. No one came snooping. It had just been us, which was exactly how we had wanted it to be.

Tunnel or no tunnel, I wouldn't ever let my guard down completely, but having the little hideout did make things feel a little more, well, safe. Of course, I was too afraid to actually say it out loud.

"I'm going to keep working," Carter said raising his eyebrows at me. He paused for a second but when we didn't leave he waved his hands shooing us away.

"You can take a break if you want to," Penn said looking at me for a second. He crossed his arms in front of his chest. "You need to sleep every so often too."

"I will. I just want to get a little more work done," Carter said as he pushed the shovel into the dirt. The scratching noise of the shovel against the earth echoed slightly in the small space.

Penn placed his hand on my back and gently guided me towards the built-in ladder. After I climbed up, I stood there watching Penn as he pulled himself into the basement with ease. His arms looked stronger, his muscles bigger, probably because of all the digging he'd been doing.

It was dark when we got back upstairs. I reached over to light the candle we kept on the table and looked out the little slit between the curtains.

The nights were long, and the winter seemed to be dragging on. There were days I wondered if it was going to last as long as it had after the big storm had taken everything from us. The first big storm, the longer winter, and the scorching temperatures seemed like they had all

28

occurred a lifetime ago. It almost felt as though it hadn't happened to me, that I'd only heard stories about it happening.

The Earth's climate had never seemed quite the same as it once was. Sometimes I wondered if HOME was playing around with whatever they had created that caused the issues in the first place or if this was just how things were now. Whatever was going on, winter was here, and it didn't seem like it was going to leave anytime soon.

"Tired?" Penn asked stopping in front of the bedroom as he looked at me over his shoulder.

I closed the curtain near the table and turned towards him. His muscular arms were stretched out over his head, grabbing on to the trim around the door.

"Yeah, I guess so. Shouldn't we wait until Carter comes up though?" I asked. I knew he had a lantern and a flashlight just in case, but I worried that if they'd both fail while we were asleep, he'd be stuck in total darkness until we woke up.

"He'll be fine. It's not the first time one of us has worked at night," Penn said with a smile. He yawned and let his arms fall down to his sides. "Come."

It seemed as though he didn't want to

go to bed without me. Maybe, somehow, I helped him fall asleep at night just as much as he had always helped me.

Penn and I often went to bed at the same time unless he was busy working on something. I slept much better when Penn was at my side.

Every night that I laid down next to him, I remembered how I had climbed into his bed back when we were inside HOME. Even then I'd felt safer next to him.

I wasn't exactly sure why, but everything felt different with Penn. Maybe it was being in this house, but it felt like there was a chance we'd actually be OK.

The room was so silent I could hear, or at least I thought I could, Carter digging deep below the house. The moon must have been bright based on the blueish tint that shone in through the spaces at the sides and the middle of the curtain.

I glanced over at Penn to see if he was sleeping, but he wasn't. He was wide awake, looking at me. When he caught my eye, he smiled but quickly looked away as if he'd been caught doing something he shouldn't have been.

"What?" I said tilting my head to the side. I tried to look into his eyes, but he seemed to be avoiding me.

"Nothing," he said but let out a small laugh.

"Tell me!"

"I was just thinking about how even with all the shit out there, HOME and stuff, that I was happy to be here with you. Well, and Carter too, of course. I can't even remember the last time I felt like this. If ever."

"Yeah," I said looking towards the window. I tried not to let myself think about those that weren't here with us. The ones that were special to me, but hadn't made it this far. "We've been through a lot together."

He propped himself up on his elbow and looked at me. I could feel his eyes on me, and he could probably tell just how close my thoughts were to drifting away from the moment, back towards all the bad memories.

"Oh shit, I'm sorry," he said placing his finger on my chin. He turned my face, so I had no choice but to look at him. "I wish things would have been different too, but things are going to be good from now on. I'll do everything I can to make sure of it. The last thing I want is for you to feel any more sadness. Any of us."

"I know," I said forcing a smile.

His eyes glowed like two bright blue moons illuminating the darkness of the room. I pushed the negative thoughts back down before they could surface any further. After all, I was happy to be here with Penn and Carter, too. It really did seem like things were finally going to be OK.

We were always going to have to worry about HOME — that wouldn't ever change. As long as they were out there, they were a threat to us, but this place, this time, maybe it really would be different.

Instead of sitting around in fear, we were doing what we could to keep ourselves safe for when they did come poking around. We weren't running, this was our place, and we were going to keep it as long as we possibly could.

"I'd do anything for you," Penn said, and something in the air changed. My heart sped up, and I breathed slowly while he held my gaze. "I owe that to you."

"You don't owe me anything. I forgave you a long time ago for all that, Penn," I said airily.

"I haven't forgiven myself." It was Penn's turn to look away from me.

32

I shook my head and smiled at him. He probably wouldn't ever forgive himself for having worked for HOME and the things he'd done when we first met. But none of that mattered anymore.

"You really don't need to beat yourself up over it," I said tilting my head down so I could look into his gorgeous glowing eyes. "It was a long time ago. You are not that person, and I know that. You know that. None of that matters to me."

"Well, it matters to me," he said gazing into my eyes.

I could see just how strongly he felt about his past. How badly he wanted to change it. He hated HOME, and he hated what he'd done for them.

He swallowed and took my hand into his. "I just want you to know what you mean to me. How much I care… the lengths I would—"

"I know. I feel the same."

He shook his head as though I didn't understand. Like I couldn't possibly feel the same thing he was feeling.

"I do," I said with a frown.

"This is different," Penn said staring back into my eyes. I wished I could read his mind. I wanted to know everything Penn

33

was thinking.

When he started leaning closer, I realized he had meant something different from what I had. I knew where his mind was and what was about to happen.

I didn't move forward, but I didn't move back either. My pulse quickened. I swallowed hard as Penn moved his lips closer to mine.

It almost surprised me when I realized I didn't want him to stop. I wanted him to kiss me.

Chapter four.

When his lips touched mine, my whole body ignited. I could feel everything he'd felt for me in that single kiss, and it was almost too much to handle.

Penn slid his hand around my neck and held me close as he kissed me harder with a need I'd never experienced before. It seemed like he had been waiting a very long time for this moment and it was everything he'd wanted and more.

I reached over and put my hand on his arm, feeling his solid muscles under my fingertips. My body temperature started to rise as if I could feel the flames from the fireplace reaching all the way from the living room into our bedroom, wrapping me in its warmth.

I sighed as I inched closer. His passion was intoxicating, and I wanted more.

He pulled back slightly and looked at me with fire in his eyes. His fingers glided softly down my back causing me to relax into him.

Penn swallowed and then smiled. "I can't believe this is happening."

"Why?" I said in a breath as I ran my fingers through his short hair. It was longer than it had once been, but he still kept it quite short.

"I just never thought it would," he said looking down at the small space between us. "It's always been you. Since the day I saw you. For me, it's been you."

I didn't know what to say. There was a time I thought Penn kind of had feelings for me, but it had been short lived. He'd known I had a boyfriend and backed off. I guess maybe he'd just never stopped feeling, he just stopped pursuing.

"Why didn't you tell me?" I asked, but I frowned at myself, knowing it was a stupid question. I already knew the answer.

"I didn't want to get in the way," he said, but I knew what he really wanted to say was that it was because at the time I'd been in a relationship. "I wanted you to be happy."

"I… I… I'm not sure what to say."

"You don't have to say anything," Penn said moving his lips closer to mine.

36

All I could think about was how long he'd had feelings for me. My heart rate increased, and my breathing felt erratic.

I pressed my lips, and then my whole body against his so hard he rolled onto his back with me on top. He ran his hand down my backside roughly as I pressed my palm against his solid chest.

I slipped my hand inside of his shirt and felt his warm, smooth skin. He felt so amazing, and I wanted more. I wanted to feel every inch of him.

When I reached down for the hem of his shirt, the creaks of Carter coming up the stairs filled the air. I reacted instantly, pulling away from Penn, but he grabbed my hips and held me tighter, not wanting to let me go.

"Carter's coming," I whispered. Penn groaned as he let go and I rolled away from him.

After a few seconds, I felt his fingers lightly touching the back of my hand. He let out a soft sigh and slowly threaded his fingers into mine.

I watched as Carter walked by the room and into the living room. The sofa squeaked as he collapsed down on top of it.

"Are you leaving?" I asked as I

chewed on one of my broken fingernails.

"Not tonight," he said softly and rolled on this side, facing me. He wrapped his arm around my middle and kissed the top of my head. "Good night, Ros."

"Night, Penn."

It didn't take him long to fall asleep. All of the work he'd been doing below the house had made both him and Carter extra tired.

I was tired too, but after what had just happened, I couldn't fall asleep. My thoughts were running wild as I tried to make sense of everything.

When I'd left the facility, getting back to Penn had been so important, had I developed feelings for him back then without realizing it? Or maybe I knew deep down, but hadn't been ready to admit it to myself. Was I really ready now?

Penn had always taken care of me, and I had no doubt that he always would. Things were different now that it was just the three of us. He didn't want to hold back anymore, and I was pretty sure I didn't want him to, even though it was all so overwhelming.

After everything Penn and I had been through, could I really allow myself to go to that place with him? Could I even allow myself to feel that way about someone again? It always seemed to end in heartache. I was really sick of losing everyone, and I wasn't sure how much more I could take.

* * *

As the days went by, Penn and Carter continued to dig the tunnel. They made tons of progress, but they still weren't sure where the tunnel would go. While they did their digging, I would watch for HOME, occasionally watching out the windows, but they never came. In fact, no one came.

We had gotten into a nice routine, and we were as close to happy as we probably would ever get. And likely as safe as we'd ever get too.

I was resting on the sofa drifting in and out of sleep when Carter walked past. He peered out the front window for several minutes before letting the curtain fall.

"It seems there might be a break in the storm," Carter said walking over to the sofa. He looked down at me but only held my gaze for a moment.

"Yeah? Well, that's good I suppose," I said blinking several times. I shifted my body back so I was sitting up more, resting my back on the armrest.

"I think I should go out on a run, replenish some of our supplies. Get back on track going through the houses, you know, get back into the swing of things," Carter said walking away.

I shook my head and swung my legs over and sat up straight. He'd definitely gotten my attention if that's what he had intended. I crossed my arms and watched Carter pacing in the kitchen.

"Did you talk to Penn about this?" I asked after a long awkward silence.

"I did."

"And?"

Carter rubbed his hands together and swallowed hard. "He was okay with it."

"Did he think it was a good idea?" I said standing up and shifting my weight back and forth, feeling uncomfortable with what they decided. They hadn't even bothered to see what I thought about the stupid idea, given we had more than enough supplies. It was still cold outside, and there was so much snow on the ground it just didn't seem like a good idea at all.

We had enough in the basement, it would last months. Not to mention we had plentiful water and could catch fish from the lake. I know they both worried that we would run out, but it wasn't like that was going to happen anytime soon.

"I really think you should wait until spring," I said picking at a fingernail. "After the snow has melted."

"We don't know if there will be a spring," Carter said his voice increasing in volume slightly. "It's not like we can just put it off indefinitely."

"It'll happen."

"Are you sure?" Carter asked putting his hands on the counter and leaning forward.

I opened my mouth as if to say something but quickly snapped it shut. I couldn't be sure there would be a spring, although I was fairly certain it would come sooner or later. But for all I knew it could take longer than usual which would definitely make Penn nervous.

Penn started walking up the stairs loudly. I didn't know if he had heard what we were talking about and I wasn't sure I wanted to have this conversation with him.

41

But the second I saw him I couldn't help but ask about it.

"You really think this is a good idea?" I said crossing my arms in front of my chest.

"Think what's a good idea?" Penn asked narrowing his eyes at me.

I shook my head back and forth slightly and threw my hand into the air. "Carter going off to get supplies. It's cold out there, and there's so much snow, can't he just wait until spring? Until it warms up some?"

Penn smiled, walked towards me carefully as though he was afraid I might explode. When I tilted my head to the side, he stopped. Maybe he could tell I was getting angry.

"He'll be fine," Penn said taking a deep breath. "It's not like I'm making him go. I said I would, but he wants to do it."

"I just want to get out of here for a while… feeling a little cooped up," Carter said looking at Penn and avoiding eye contact with me.

"It just doesn't seem like the best idea," I said rubbing my hand on my forehead, knowing this wasn't an argument I was going to win.

"Three days," Carter said finally

glancing at me. "Four tops."

I lowered my head and sighed. "Let the record show I was against this idea."

"Noted," Carter said with a smile. He walked over to me and put his hand on my shoulder. He rubbed it back and forth while bending down to look into my eyes. "Who knew you'd worry so much about me?"

"I worry about both of you," I said feeling the tension in my forehead.

"I've done this same thing multiple times. This isn't going to be any different, well, maybe a little colder," Carter said giving my shoulder a slight squeeze. "I'll be fine. Besides this will give you and Penn some alone time."

"We don't need alone time," I said looking back and forth between Penn and Carter.

A knowing smile appeared on Carter's face, and it made my cheeks hot. "If I wasn't going, Penn would. It was my turn, and I want to go. I need to go. All I've been doing is digging and sleeping, I need to get out of this place, just for a few days."

I sighed and looked at Penn. It wasn't like I wanted either of them to go. There was no impending need for them to go, but it wasn't like I could force either of them to stay.

"Whatever," I said walking over to the sofa, sitting down heavily.

Penn hadn't said much about the whole thing, but he did seem to think it would be OK. If Penn thought it would be fine, perhaps I shouldn't worry so much. It wasn't like he wanted anything bad to happen to Carter either.

"If you aren't back in four days, I'm going to go out there to look for you. I'll go myself if I have to," I said, mostly looking at Penn.

"Maybe make it five days," Carter said with a smile.

"Four," I said staring at my knees. I wasn't going to let them change my mind.

"I'll leave in the morning," he said as he turned and walked out of the room. The stairs creaked as he made his way downstairs, and I had to hope it was to pack his bag, rather than to do more digging.

Penn sat down on the opposite end of the sofa. He could tell I wanted space.

"Really, he'll be fine. We've been doing this for quite some time now," Penn said.

"Not in winter," I said not wanting to

look at him.

"If it's bad, he'll come—"

"What if there's a blizzard or something," I said shaking my head.

Penn scooted over just a few inches closer. "I talked to him about it. He'll know what to do to get back. I'll make sure he's prepared as best as he can be."

"I still think it's a terrible idea. Things can go wrong, you know that," I said, but I was done arguing about it. I was outnumbered and Carter was going to do it no matter what I said.

"It's just a little break. He knows how to take care of himself."

I couldn't help but wonder if this was just how it was going to be now. When Carter got back, was Penn going to go? What they should have been doing is figuring out a way for us to be less dependent on getting supplies from out there, because eventually they'd be gone.

What were they even hoping to find? We had all the fish we could catch, unlimited water and in the spring we would be able to grow our own vegetables. We had guns, clothing… anything we could possibly need we probably had it. In fact, we probably had several.

I already knew why. Penn would always want more, and apparently, Carter was on board.

I stood up and started walking towards the bedroom. Penn didn't ask where I was going or why I wasn't waiting for him. He knew I wasn't happy, and while I wasn't angry at him, I just wanted to be alone so I could think. I needed some time to process the fact that Carter was going out on a run, even though he probably shouldn't.

I didn't close the door, but I laid down on the bed and stared at the curtain. Maybe I overreacted. Carter knew what he was doing, and he could take care of himself.

I wish he would wait longer, but he probably would be fine. It wasn't like I could blame him for having cabin fever, I had experienced it back in the shelter. And even after what I had been through with the facility, sometimes I felt it too.

He'd be OK. I just had to keep telling myself that. He would be OK.

Chapter five.

It had been three days since Carter left, and I was hoping he'd walk across the front yard any minute. He had another day of travel allotted, but I couldn't help but frequently look out of the window hoping he'd return early.

My anxiety was starting to get the better of me. I was worried about all the things that could have gone wrong. Carter could come back empty handed for all I cared, as long as he came back.

"Relax," Penn said as he flipped through some old hunting magazine I'd seen him look through at least a hundred times. "He'll be back tomorrow."

"Maybe he misses us," I said stepping away from the window and letting the curtain fall. I sat down next to Penn, and he put his arm around my shoulders.

"He probably does," Penn said pulling me closer so he could kiss the top of my head. "But he'd mentioned something about giving us some time to be alone if I recall correctly."

I crossed my arms and scrunched up my face. "Yeah, what was that all about anyway? What makes him think we need, like, this special alone time?"

Penn set the magazine down on the end-table. He took my hand into his.

"Don't get mad but—"

"Buuuut?"

"I may have mentioned that I had some feelings for you to Carter."

I turned to the side and narrowed my eyes at him. "So, you told him to leave?"

"No, of course not. That was completely unrelated. I told him I was going to go on a run, and he said he wanted to go, but that was like weeks after I told him I had feelings for you."

"Oh," I said still not knowing exactly how I should feel about everything. My feelings for Penn grew every day, or maybe I just realized they were there more each day, but he'd known for a while. At the same time, it was hard to forget what happened to anyone I ever cared about, and I didn't want that to happen to Penn.

"He said he had already pretty much figured it out anyway, so it wasn't like I was revealing a deep, dark secret."

"He knew?"

Penn grinned at me and pulled me closer even though I kept my body stiff. "Apparently, I don't hide it as well as I thought. Then again, he saw how crazy I got when you were missing and stuck at that stupid facility."

I nodded and let my body relax against his. There was no way I could deny how safe I felt in his arms.

"So what I think," Penn said with a huge grin, "is that we should enjoy this time we have alone together while it lasts. Carter will be back tomorrow, and all you've done since he left was pace the living room and look out the curtains. Maybe I should be jealous."

"Funny. I'm just worried about him."

"It hasn't snowed. The weather hasn't changed. He's fine. Carter knows what he's doing, he's done it a hundred times," Penn said placing his finger at the bottom of my chin, forcing me to look at him. "I really, really don't want to talk about Carter anymore."

Penn slowly moved his lips towards mine. When he was a couple inches away, I closed my eyes and let out a soft breath.

I wanted him to kiss me, but my body was tense from the stress and anxiety. I was filled with so much worry that I wasn't sure if I could relax enough to be in the moment with Penn the way I wanted to.

When his lips touched mine, I melted. I was safe. All my worry and anxiety drifted away. Every time he kissed me, I could feel everything thing he'd ever felt for me surge through that kiss, and it was powerful… intoxicating… overwhelming.

I wasn't sure who I was denying my feelings to, mostly myself I guess, but I couldn't do it any longer. My feelings for Penn were clear, and I was ready to give into them.

It seemed as though everyone already knew about them anyway, so why fight it. I already knew life was short, might as well enjoy what life I had left.

I wrapped my arms around Penn and pulled him down on top of me. My hands worked to feel every inch of his body.

"Wow," Penn said with a huge grin. "What's gotten into you?"

"Want me to stop?" I asked with a raised eyebrow. I smirked and shifted away slightly.

Penn grabbed me tighter. "Most.

Definitely. Not," he said as he placed kisses down the side of my neck. "I just hope I don't wake up from this dream."

Penn's fingers gripped the hem of my shirt and with a quick movement, pulled it up and over my head. My body warmed as he touched and kissed every inch of my exposed skin.

I twisted my fingers into his hair and let out a soft sigh. Being with him felt so perfect. So right. Like it was always how it was supposed to be.

His touch activated me like nothing else. It felt like I was going to melt into the sofa.

When he slid his hand between us and popped the button on my jeans, I squeaked. He glanced at me, but I just smiled as if it hadn't happened. I had no intentions of stopping him, it had only taken me by surprise for a split second.

"OK?" he asked, and I nodded. Everything was more than OK.

When he saw the expression on my face, it didn't take him more than a couple seconds to undress me. His clothes were off even faster.

Our hands were everywhere as we tangled ourselves into one. Penn's body was silky, solid and I couldn't get enough.

Time seemed to stand still. My body lightened as all the stress and anxiety was replaced with passion and desire.

Our bodies moved in perfect rhythm, and together we went to an amazing place where only Penn and I existed. It was a place where nothing bad could ever happen, and everything was always perfect.

I wrapped my legs around him as he buried his face in my hair, our bodies rocking into one another.

My head rolled back, and Penn's muscles tightened. I could feel his heart pounding against my skin.

I couldn't stop smiling as we floated back down to earth. Both of us breathing together, slowing as it returned to normal.

Penn leaned back and smiled at me as he traced a line down the side of my face with his fingertip. I pulled his lips closer to mine and kissed him.

"That was incredible," he said looking at me through his heavy eyelids. "I don't think I could be any happier than I am at this moment."

It was all mushy and overly gushy, but I felt the exact same way. Being with Penn had just felt so right.

"Yeah," I said, my voice raspy. "But I should really get dressed."

"Why?" he said looking at me with a small smirk.

"In case he comes back," I said, and I could feel all the last drops of our passion leave the room. More like I'd pushed them out of the room.

Penn lowered his head for a second but then pulled on his boxers and jeans. I could tell he hadn't wanted to think about Carter. At least not at that moment.

"Well, it's not like we want to be lying around like this when he returns," I said biting my lip. "He'd turn around and go right back out there again."

Penn nodded as he leaned back against the sofa. Once I had my T-shirt on, he patted the cushion next to him.

I curled up on the sofa and snuggled into his arm. He sighed as he rested his head on the top of mine.

Even though I was worried about Carter, I drifted off into a blissful rest. When I woke up, my head was on the armrest, and Penn was pacing in front of the window.

"Something wrong?" I asked hugging my knees to my chest.

Penn looked at me and forced a smile. "No, I guess there was a part of me that was hoping he'd be back today too."

"I thought you weren't worried?" I asked.

"I didn't think I was, but then I couldn't sleep. Kept having terrible thoughts."

I bit my cheek and pulled nervously at my fingers. "What should we do?"

"There's nothing we can do. We wait. I'm sure he'll be back tomorrow. That was the plan."

I got up off of the sofa and tried to look out the window, but Penn blocked my way. It wasn't like it would change anything if I peeked just for a second.

"He's not here. I just looked."

I let out a big sigh as I crossed my arms.

"Let's get something to eat, then go to bed," Penn said wrapping an arm around my shoulders as he led me towards the kitchen. There was something about the way he said 'bed' that sent a tingle up and down my spine.

Penn had collected a fish from the icebox we kept on the porch. It was filled with snow to keep the fish fresh.

After he finished cooking the fish, I prepared some rice. We ate the warm meal next to the fire. Occasionally we shared a smile, but other than that we didn't really talk. I couldn't help but wonder if his thoughts were as much on Carter as mine were.

After we finished eating, he moved closer. When he started kissing my neck, I was sure his mind was on only one thing. Me.

He took my hand and flashed me a sexy smirk before he led me into the bedroom.

Chapter six.

When I woke up, I wasn't sure if it was morning. It had been a restless sleep… it felt as though I hadn't slept at all.

The room was lighter, but it wasn't its usual pale yellow from the sun. Instead, the walls were tinged with a dreary, light gray color.

"Penn?" I said softly as I placed my hand on the other side of the bed. But I only felt the cool sheets. Penn wasn't there.

It didn't take long for me to recognize the faint digging noises that came from somewhere deep below. He'd gone down to work.

I wondered how long he'd been busy digging. In fact, I wondered if he had even slept at all.

Maybe after we had been together, he waited until I fell asleep so he could sneak away to work on the tunnels? If he was as worried about Carter as I was, he'd do that

56

to keep his mind occupied.

I rolled out of bed with a groan and walked over to the window. It was surprising I hadn't slept better considering everything that had happened with Penn. Maybe I'd had nightmares I couldn't remember? I'd probably been worried about Carter even in my sleep.

I stuck my finger between the curtains and pulled them slightly apart. It was hard to tell how long it had been going on, but there was a buildup along the windowsill. I couldn't even see any of the tracks in the snow that had been made when Penn gathered wood for the fireplace.

"Dammit," I said as I watched a thick snowflake land on the glass. It stuck there for a few seconds before it slowly started to melt.

The snow falling was thick and heavy... I couldn't see as far as I would have liked. If Carter was out there traveling in this snow storm, he could easily get lost.

"Penn!" I shouted. When I turned to leave the room, I slammed into something that shouldn't have been there and screamed.

I blinked several times before realizing it was just Penn standing there.

He'd come upstairs, but apparently, I hadn't heard him come into the room.

There was no mistaking the worried look on his face. He must have seen the winter storm outside our window.

I sucked in a deep breath to calm my racing heart. "Did you look outside the—"

"Yes," Penn said glancing at the window. "Still coming down?"

"Yeah," I said unable to keep the worried expression off my face.

"A lot?"

"Yeah." I frowned.

Penn slammed his fist down on the dresser causing everything on it, and on the wall behind it, to rattle. He walked past me and stomped to the curtain. It was as though he just had to see for himself.

"Dammit."

Penn started pacing as he ran his hand through his hair. After a minute or so he stopped in the doorway and glanced at me over his shoulder.

"Going back down," he said without meeting my eyes.

"What? Wait! Shouldn't we do something?" I said shaking my head.

"Like what?"

I swallowed down a hard lump in my

throat and squeezed my eyes shut as I tried to think of something… anything we could do. There had to be something, but I only had one idea, and I already knew he'd shoot it down.

"We could go out to look—"

"No," Penn said cutting his hand sharply through the air. "Then we'd all be out there wandering around getting lost. We wait. He's probably just waiting for the storm to pass."

"But, Penn, we really should do…."

He turned his face away from me. "He's probably holed up somewhere, warm next to a fire. He'll be back. We just need to give him a little extra time."

I cautiously walked closer, and when I gently placed my hand on his shoulder, he looked down towards his feet. My heart rate started to increase, I was pretty sure I wouldn't be able to change his mind.

"What if you're wrong?" I asked.

"It's a chance we have to take. At least for now. We can't go out there and get lost too. Imagine if he came back right after we'd left."

"Well, we'd leave him a note of course."

Penn shook his head slowly as if he

was considering it. "He'd still come out after us. Maybe not right away, but he would. Let's give it a few more days. We're probably just worried about nothing."

"At least you admit you're worried," I muttered.

He stepped away, and my hand dropped down to my side. My blood started to feel warm and not in a good way. I was angry. I'd been right. Carter should never have gone out on the run.

I sucked in a big breath. "If he's not back in two days, I'll go myself."

Penn stopped abruptly, but before he could turn to say anything to me, I slammed the bedroom door shut. As far as I was concerned, the conversation was over.

It felt as though I could still feel his presence on the other side of the door, but if he was there, he didn't bother to knock. He didn't try to argue. Penn didn't say anything at all.

I lay down on the bed and tried not to think of all the things that could have gone wrong. It wasn't like Carter wasn't capable of taking care of himself, he was, but that didn't make me feel any better. Things didn't always go according to plan. He could have succumbed to the cold, or worse,

HOME could have found him. For some reason, I kept imagining him lying there in the snow, frozen to death.

It was probably about twenty minutes later when I heard the digging noises start up again. Even though it was faint, I could tell Penn was digging fast. Apparently, he was taking his aggressions out on the dirt below.

* * *

It didn't surprise me when, after two more days had gone by, Penn was down digging before I even work up. I was pretty sure he was avoiding me.

Penn knew I wouldn't leave without talking to him first, so he was hiding. He was delaying things because he didn't want me going out after Carter, but of course, I was going to go with or without him.

Instead of going down to talk to him, to try to convince him, I started packing my things. After I dug one of the other backpacks out of the closet, I walked over to the window. Maybe, just maybe, Carter would just happen to be walking towards the house. It wasn't like I wanted to go out searching for him, but I had to do something.

What if going was the wrong thing to do? Maybe Penn was right about waiting here for him. When I'd gone missing, Carter stayed here while Penn went out searching. The only problem with that plan was if I suggested it, I don't think Penn would ever leave my side. It would have to be something very important for him to ' leave me. Something that threatened our lives if he didn't.

I pulled open the curtains, and when I saw the shape of a person, I smiled. My hand was inches away from tapping on the glass to get their attention, only I noticed at the last second. The person outside wasn't Carter.

I carefully put the curtains into place before I took a step back. My breaths were sharp and made my chest feel tight. I started to feel lightheaded.

I didn't want to take my eyes off of the man, but I had to get Penn. The digging noises suddenly seemed as though they were at least twenty times louder than they had been before. I couldn't help but wonder if the man outside could hear them.

My eyes were glued to the curtain as I clumsily backed away towards the basement door. Once my feet touched the tiled kitchen floor, I turned around and bolted down the stairs.

When I got to the bottom, Penn was deep inside the tunnel they'd started digging. I put my hand on the opening and tried to catch my breath.

Penn turned to look at me, and he could instantly tell something was wrong. He dropped his shovel and walked several feet towards me into the little storage area they'd dug.

"What's wrong," he asked looking into my eyes. He probably thought it had something to do with Carter.

"A man," I said taking a breath between each word. "Outside."

His eyes narrowed. "Here?"
"Yes!"

Penn pushed past me and climbed up the ladder steps faster than I would have thought possible. It was the first time I'd been alone in the hideout area, and for some reason, it gave me the chills, and not just because it was cooler underground.

I climbed up and found Penn walking from window to window. He barely stopped to glance at me as he moved around.

"I don't see anyone," he whispered.

"He was out front," I said pointing to the window where I had spotted the man.

Penn went back to the window but shook his head. He walked over and stood next to me before bending down. Penn looked into my eyes as if he was searching for something.

"What was he doing out there?" Penn asked, and I knew his switch had flipped. He was in his super-ninja-military ex-HOME mode.

"Just walking," I said shaking my head slightly. "I didn't watch him long. Sort of freaked out and ran to get you."

"Hmm," Penn said gently moving me against the wall next to the sofa before walking into the bedroom. Even though I couldn't hear what he was doing, I knew he was looking out of the window.

I waited for what felt like a long time, but Penn didn't come out of the room. Instead of calling out for him, I quietly stepped inside the bedroom.

"Get back!" Penn scolded in a whisper-quiet voice. I could tell by the look on his face, and how he was hiding behind the curtain, he'd located the man.

I quickly stepped back into the living room and squeezed my eyes shut. My heart started to race even faster than it already had been. Something about Penn seeing the man made it feel even more real… more threatening.

After a few seconds, Penn zipped past me, checking his gun as he walked by. "Stay here," he said holding the gun close to his chest. "Don't move."

"Penn… what are you doing?"

"I said, stay here," he said annunciating each word as though he didn't think I had understood them the first time.

"You can't go out there!" I said feeling my hands tighten into fists.

Penn pulled back the curtain and checked before he put his hand on the doorknob. He looked at me one more time, and even though I didn't want him to go, I nodded. Then he was gone, and I was alone, not knowing what was happening.

Penn had quickly opened and closed the door without making any noise. I sucked in a deep breath before I ran to the window.

Chapter seven.

I peeled back the curtain, but I didn't see either Penn or the man. The room was so quiet, my ears started to buzz.

My eyes were glued to the empty yard. I wanted to move to another window to check for them, but I was afraid to move. Fear of what I might see was holding me in place.

I closed my eyes, hoping the buzzing would stop and I could hear something, but it only made the noise in my ears louder. Tears started to fill my eyes, as my emotions were overloaded... stress, anxiety, worry about Penn when I already felt all those things about what was going on with Carter.

I put my hand on the wall trying to push against it, trying to force myself to move. Maybe I'd be able to see Penn outside the bedroom, only I had to get there first.

I wrapped my arms around my middle as I felt a cold shiver run up and down my spine. It felt odd to feel so chilly when there was a fire blazing in the fireplace only a few feet away from where I stood.

Each foot felt as though it weighed twenty pounds as I tried to move them towards the bedroom. I stopped in my tracks when I was about halfway there. A loud gunshot rang out, causing the noise in my ears to cease.

My feet were suddenly free of their weight. It was as though they had a mind of their own as they brought me to my nightstand. I pulled open the drawer and didn't hesitate to grab my gun Penn insisted on keeping there when I didn't have it on me.

The cool metal always felt strange in my hand. It was a necessity to have one, but I'd never get used to it the way Penn was.

Before I knew it, I was walking out the front door. Snowflakes landed on my face and stuck to my clothing. I barely even noticed how cold it was.

I opened my mouth to call out for Penn, but I quickly snapped it shut. What if it wasn't Penn that would answer me? What if the gunshot hadn't come from Penn's gun?

If anything happened to Penn, I didn't

think I could handle it. In fact, I was sure I couldn't. It would definitely throw me into some downward spiral I probably didn't want to think about while I was outside looking for him.

I pushed the thoughts out of my mind and slowly looked around the side of the house. Nothing.

I kept moving, scanning the area, but all I could see was the snow, and the fence Penn and Carter hadn't gotten around to finishing. I wasn't even sure it would make a difference if they had. If someone wanted to get inside our property, they'd find a way.

I looked around the house into the backyard. Penn was crouched down next to the man that had been wandering around our yard. His feet were stiffly pointed towards the sky, and I knew, without a doubt, he was dead.

Penn spun around abruptly with his gun pointed directly at me. He quickly dropped it to his side when he realized it was only me.

"Shit, sorry," Penn said turning his attention back to the man lying on the ground. "Told you to stay inside."

I swallowed hard and let out the breath I'd inadvertently been holding.

"Yeah, well, I heard the gunshot."

"Mmm-hmm," Penn said flipping something back and forth in his hand.

"What is that?" I asked, cautiously stepping up next to him, tucking my gun into my waistband. When I got a little closer, I could see the bullet hole right in the middle of the man's forehead. Deadly accuracy.

"Have you seen this before?" Penn said pressing something into the palm of my hand.

I opened my hand and looked down at a tiny, delicate cross on a chain. It didn't look like something a man would wear, and in this world, it definitely wasn't worth anything.

"I don't think so," I said squinting at the necklace. "Why?"

"I could swear I've seen it before, maybe Carter?"

"I never saw Carter wearing a necklace like this. Looks kind of feminine," I said shaking my head and handing the chain back to Penn.

He looked it over again and tucked it into his pocket as he stood up. "Come on," Penn said taking my hand and leading me back towards the front of the house. "I'll take care of this once you're back inside."

"I could help," I said with a shrug.

Penn shook his head, and I rolled my eyes. It wasn't worth arguing over since it wasn't an argument I'd win.

As we walked to the house, I couldn't stop thinking about the necklace. There must have been a reason that Penn thought it belonged to Carter.

"Why did you think that was Carter's necklace?" I said stopping in front of him before he could open the front door.

"When you were gone, he was always holding something, I asked him one time what it was, and he just said it was Alice's. I never got a really good look at it, but if I had to bet money…" Penn said tapping his pocket. He stepped around me, opened the door and gestured for me to go inside.

I couldn't remember if I'd ever seen Alice with the necklace on, but of all the things Carter had with him, why would the man have taken the necklace? Maybe he'd just liked it, or maybe it wasn't all he'd taken. Maybe it was all he had with him.

"What did you say to the man?" I asked before Penn could close the door.

"Nothing."

"Nothing? You just shot him?"

"Yes," Penn said and started to close the door.

I put my hand out and stopped it. "What if that is Carter's? How sure are you that it could be his?"

"Pack your things," Penn said, and he placed his hand on top of mine. He peeled it off the door and kissed it before he closed it.

I could hear the crunch of snow get fainter through the wooden door as he walked away. "Already did."

Chapter eight.

I was lying in bed staring at the ceiling when Penn finally made his way to the bedroom. He had taken his time to come to the bed, which was unusual, but I wasn't going to ask him about it.

It had taken him awhile to deal with the body, and after he was finished, he took a long bath. When he finished that, he insisted on replacing the water he used, but I thought it was an excuse. It felt as though maybe he was avoiding me.

He stood in the doorway, and I could tell from the corner of my eye he was looking at me. When I didn't say anything, he turned to the window and sucked in a deep breath.

"We'll leave in the morning," he said as he walked around the bed and sat down on his side. I heard the familiar clink-clank of his gun being set down on the nightstand. "Did you pack?"

"Yes," I said almost too softly. I

cleared my voice. "I did."

"What's wrong?" Penn asked turning his head ever so slightly to the side, but I kept my gaze focused on the ceiling.

"Just worried."

Penn didn't say anything. The room felt extra quiet until he let out a long sigh. "Me too."

I felt like crying, but I bit my cheek so I wouldn't. If Penn was worried that meant things were bad. Penn rarely let his worry show, it was probably part of the training he had at HOME, but since he was, things had to be bad.

"I'm just so sick and tired of all this," I said unable to stop my voice from cracking. I sniffed and focused my eyes hard at a spot on the ceiling. I was refusing to let the tears fall.

It was just one thing after the other, and I didn't want to lose anyone else. This world wasn't going to ease up on us until it took each one of us out of it.

Penn lay down next to me and pulled me into his arm. He stroked my hair softly.

"It's going to be OK," he said, but I was pretty sure he didn't even believe his own words. "As long as I'm alive, I won't let anything happen to you."

"That doesn't help Carter," I said swallowing hard. "I just don't know if I can take it. We keep losing everyone. If Carter's gone too, that just leaves us. Doesn't seem like very good odds to me!"

He pressed his head down against mine and held me tighter. I could feel his heart beating, pounding hard against his chest.

"We'll do everything we can to find him," Penn said.

"And what if we don't find him?"

"We will."

I shook my head and turned slightly so I could look into his eyes. "How can you be so sure?"

"We've taken the same route how many times now?"

"What if he's not on the route?" I said, my words came out much harsher than I intended.

Something could have happened to cause him to leave the route. Penn knew that.

He looked away from me, and I knew it was because he didn't have an answer. It was like he didn't want to think about the other possibilities.

"Let's just try to get some sleep.

74

We'll need it for tomorrow," Penn said and kissed the top of my head.

I let out a heavy sigh, and Penn ignored it. He probably didn't know what to say. There probably wasn't even anything he could say. In fact, I was pretty sure he was just as worried and frustrated as I was, but of course, he was far better at hiding it.

It wasn't like I was angry or frustrated with Penn, so I hoped he didn't feel as though I was taking it out on him. I was just upset that Carter had even gone on the run in the first place. He never should have left. I should have done more to discourage him from leaving.

Perhaps on some level, Penn felt guilty. He didn't do anything to stop Carter from going, in fact, he had kind of encouraged it.

Penn would have been the one to go if Carter hadn't, or at least it had seemed that way. It was hard to know if Penn would have actually gone when it came down to it.

I tried to force myself to get some sleep because Penn was right, I would need to be at the top of my game. It was going to be a long hike through the snow, and I wasn't sure how my mostly healed injury would hold up.

My side where I'd suffered the rib injury hadn't returned to normal, and I was pretty sure it never would. It wasn't like that mattered though, I wasn't going to let that stop me from looking for Carter.

I closed my eyes and let my body relax into Penn's. If there was one thing I believed, it was that Penn wouldn't let anything happen to me while he was alive. He would do whatever it took, and I would try to do the same for him. I might as well sleep while I was here nestled in his arm as safe as we could be inside our home.

Penn's breathing was deep and slow. Either he was asleep, or he was doing an awfully good job pretending to be.

His feelings for me were so strong I could reach out and touch them, even while he rested. Maybe they'd always been there, but now that it was out in the open I couldn't ignore it.

He would protect me and keep me safe unlike anyone else ever would. I should have been able to find comfort in that, but not knowing where Carter was made it difficult.

I wrapped my arm around his middle and closed my eyes. It didn't take long before I, too, was breathing deeply.

* * *

The snow was still falling when we left in the morning, but it was far lighter than it had been. I was wearing two layers of clothing, and even though the air was cold against my face, the rest of my body was quite toasty.

Penn tilted his head to the side as he looked me over. He reached out and adjusted my backpack so it was perfectly centered on my back. He turned, locked the door behind us and nodded.

"OK. Ready?" Penn asked looking into my eyes. It almost looked as though he was hoping I'd change my mind. Beg him to stay. Not because he didn't want to find Carter, but because he didn't want anything to happen to me.

"Yes," I said straightening my shoulders.

"Did you leave a note?"

"Yes."

Penn grabbed my hand and led me away from the house. Neither of us talked as we made our way through the snow and across the front yard.

When we were next to the fence, he turned around, squinting at something.

"What is it?" I asked with a raised eyebrow.

"Nothing. Well, not nothing exactly," he said facing forward again. "We're leaving tracks in the snow."

I didn't bother to look. It wasn't like there was anything we could do about it.

"Maybe the snow will cover them," I said looking up at the sky. I blinked rapidly when a snowflake landed on my eyelash.

"Hmm, yes, maybe," Penn said, but he sounded unsure. With how little snow was falling at this point, it would take all day for the snow to cover our tracks.

As we walked in silence, my thoughts drifted to Carter. Where was he? Something had to have gone wrong. Why wasn't Penn freaking out more? Was he just that worried about something happening to me? There was just no way Carter would have stayed away from us this long, at least not by his choice.

Maybe the facility had found him, just like they had found me. If he had been outnumbered, he wouldn't have had any choice. They would have taken him back to the building, and he'd be stuck inside, or maybe since he was male, they would have brought him somewhere else.

I wasn't sure I could find my way back to the facility, in fact, I was pretty sure I couldn't. Most of my memories of travel after leaving the facility were a blur because of the pain I'd been in.

Carter could get away from them just as I had, but it would take time. Although, since he knew what had happened to me, he probably wouldn't befriend anyone there that could help him escape as I had. Because of my experience, he wouldn't have been able to trust anyone at all.

No matter how hard I tried not to think about Carter being at the facility, the more vivid the images in my mind became. It was as though I suddenly couldn't picture him being anywhere but the HOME facility. And anything connected to HOME was the last place any of us, including Carter, wanted to be.

The cold air made the tears welling up in my eyes sting. It felt like tiny little icicles had formed and were stabbing my eyelids.

I wasn't exactly sure when it happened, but my pace had slowed. Penn definitely noticed.

His gaze met mine, and I could see the concern filling his narrowed eyes. "What's wrong?" he asked as he stood in front of me, blocking the way. "We don't have to keep going. We can turn back whenever you want."

"No, we can't, Penn! Don't you want to find Carter?"

"Of course I do, but—"

"I'm fine. We have to go. It's just the facility."

"What about it?" Penn asked.

"I just can't stop thinking about that place," I said the words between awkward breaths. It felt as though I was about to have an anxiety attack. If I did Penn definitely would take me back home.

It wasn't like I wanted to think about the facility, I didn't, but when I did, I couldn't help but relive the whole experience. Being trapped. Feeling like I was going to die. The fear. The pain.

"Let's go back. Carter knows the way home. If he comes back, he's going to expect us to be there," Penn said wrapping his fingers around my upper arm.

"*If* he comes back?"

Penn squeezed his eyes shut tightly and opened them again. "I didn't mean it like that."

"We left a note."

"How long do you think he'll wait before he thinks something happened to us?" Penn asked with wide eyes.

I shook my head. We had to go. Not going wasn't an option. I just had to make sure I didn't let my thoughts drift back to that place.

"I'm going. But I guess you can go back if you want to."

"Don't be ridiculous, Ros. You don't even know the way to go," Penn said crossing his arms.

I looked into his eyes so he could see just how serious I was. "I'm going. I don't want to lose anyone else. Carter might be out there somewhere. He might need us," I said taking a deep breath as I pulled back my shoulders.

I took all the memories of what I'd been through and shoved them deep down inside. They'd fit right next to all the other painful memories I stored there. Hiding all those feelings away had worked this long, what was a few more terrible memories to stockpile along with the others?

It looked like Penn wanted to pick me up and carry me back to our home. I could tell he wasn't just worried about Carter.

"Geez, Penn. I'm fine! Really," I said with a forced smile. "Let's just keep going. Please."

Penn stared at me for a moment before he nodded and led the way through the trees. I didn't have to ask to know that Penn was taking me their usual route. He walked with such confidence that I didn't have a single doubt he knew exactly where we were.

My eyes darted around the area. I was hoping to find some clue, a sign that Carter was OK. But the world around us was just white-covered trees... no clues... no signs.

We'd only been walking maybe twenty minutes when Penn stopped abruptly. He stuck his arms out in front of me protectively.

I looked around, but I didn't notice what it was that had caused him to stop. Penn tilted his head to the side as though he was listening to something.

"What are you—"

"Shh!" he said sharply.

Penn quickly pushed me behind a tree and pressed his body to mine. He was practically standing on top of me.

Then I heard it too. Voices.
Someone was coming.

Chapter nine.

When the voices got louder, Penn pointed at me and then up towards the top of the tree. I shook my head, but his eyes widened, as he pointed more aggressively.

He put his hands around my waist and gave me a boost. I reached up and grabbed the closest branch.

It was hard, but I used all the strength I had to pull myself up. Once I had my feet on the lowest branch, it was easier to climb higher. I didn't even need to look down to know that Penn was right behind me.

As the branches thinned and began to feel weak, I stopped climbing and held still. Penn came up behind me and pressed himself against my body, holding me tight against the tree.

"Shh," he whispered into my ear, but he didn't need to. I had no plans to make even the smallest of sounds if I could help it.

As the men moved closer, their voices became clearer. When they came into view, my heart started to pound so hard against my chest I was sure that they could hear it down below.

There wasn't a single doubt in my mind... the men below were from HOME. Four men, all wearing the same bright red uniform we'd seen before.

"This spot definitely isn't going to work," the tallest man said. "Not nearly enough space."

"Hmm, agreed," a slender man said as he pushed up his glasses and stiffened his spine.

They were so close I could hear the snow crunching underneath their feet as they moved around the area. If they came any closer to our tree, I was sure they'd see us.

"Course, we could cut down some of these trees if we wanted to. Always need more wood," a stocky man said. He put his hand on his hip as he turned in a slow circle surveying the area.

The slender army man rubbed his chin and looked up towards the treetops. I stopped breathing. If he saw us, he gave no indication that he had.

"Hmm, let's just keep looking," the slender man with glasses said. "We'll find something."

"We have to stay within a certain distance though," the stocky one said.

One of the men with them didn't say anything. He just stood there behind the stocky one rubbing his fingers together. It looked as though he didn't want to be there and I couldn't say I blamed him.

"I think this is totally unnecessary," the tall one said.

"Our job is to find a place," the slender one said. "And that's what we're going to do. Understood?"

"Of course, but the resistance has been eradicated, everyone is gone. This just seems unnecessary is all I'm saying," the tall one said shaking his head. The nervous looking one nodded his head slightly. "Who's going to want to stay out here and live at this camp alone?"

The slender man with glasses turned sharply to face him. His expression was slathered with annoyance. "Folks always sign up, just like at the other towers," he said pushing his glasses up his nose. "This won't be any different."

"It's all about expanding," the stocky man said slapping the taller man on the back. "And catching the strays."

The stocky one pointed two fingers at

the quiet one as if he was demonstrating what he'd do if he caught a stray. He jerked his fingers back as he mouthed what looked like the word 'pop.'

"Let's keep moving," the slender man said. "Wasting too much time here."

"Further east?" the stocky one asked.

The slender man nodded, and they all turned to leave the area. As they walked away, the quiet one turned back and looked at the tree with his head cocked to the side.

I held my breath, but it hadn't seemed as though he'd noticed us hiding there. If he had, surely he would have done something. At the very least he would have told the others.

After they were all out of view, Penn and I stayed in the tree, barely moving. I was afraid if we climbed down, they'd be at the bottom hiding, just waiting for us. Maybe Penn was worried about the same thing.

We'd probably been up there for at least twenty minutes when I felt brave enough to say something. "Do you think they're gone?" I asked in a voice quieter than a whisper. I'd been so quiet, I wasn't even sure he'd heard me. "Penn?"

"Yeah," he said, but he didn't move.

"Not sure."

In the distance, I could hear what sounded like the rumble of an engine of some kind. It sounded like something bigger than a car, but it quickly faded away, until the only thing I could hear was the slight creaking of the branches.

"Let's go," Penn said as he carefully lowered himself down to the next branch. He paused and looked as though he was waiting for something to happen, but when nothing did he continued.

Every once in a while, he'd place his hand on my back to let me know he was still there with me. But it made things only slightly more comforting. HOME having been so close to us, made me feel jittery.

When we got to the bottom, Penn looked around the area cautiously with his hand on his gun. He looked like he was in the wild west preparing for a duel.

After several minutes his hand and shoulders relaxed. He stood there staring into the distance with his head turned slightly to the side. It seemed as though he wasn't sure if we should move.

"What do you think they were doing?" I asked.

"Looking for a place to expand."

"If they come here to build, we'll have no chance, not even if the tunnel was finished," I said as a chill ran down my spine. Maybe we never had a chance anyway. Our timers were ticking ever since the first raindrop smacked me on the head.

Penn took my hand and started leading me away. He looked at the ground, and I knew he was thinking about how lucky we were that they hadn't seen us, or our tracks.

"I'd rather die than be captured by HOME again," I said after a long pause.

"Don't say—"

"It's true. It's one-hundred percent true. I won't. I won't let it happen, no way. Not again," I said looking into his eyes. I hoped he could see just how serious I was.

Penn turned his body towards mine and stared into my eyes. He took my hands into his and breathed heavily. I couldn't tell if he was angry with my words, or about HOME having been here.

"I won't let them take you." He swallowed hard and started walking again. "The good news is they don't know about us, or our place."

"How can you be so sure?"

Penn chuckled softly. "They were

this close to our house yet they didn't go check it out? Yeah, they have no clue anyone is there."

"Well, that's good, until they build whatever they plan to build. This is far too close to us. We can't have them as neighbors," I said shaking my head.

"They didn't like the location. Let's hope they build far away from here," Penn said looking up at the sky. "What we need to do, for now, is stay focused. We need to find Carter and get back."

There wasn't anything we could do to stop HOME's expansions. But hopefully, we wouldn't have to worry about it.

"Thanks to HOME we're behind schedule," Penn said as he picked up his pace.

"I didn't know we had a schedule," I said with a half-smile.

"You didn't?" he smirked right back. Of course, with Penn, there would be a schedule. "Do you know me at all?"

I laughed but abruptly stopped myself when I worried it might be too loud. It was as though it was echoing through the trees and if it carried too far, maybe HOME would hear me.

As I followed Penn through the trees

and snow, my legs started to feel heavy. It was quite clear I wasn't used to walking in the snow, or maybe it was just that I wasn't used to walking as much as we had. I didn't realize how quickly I'd get tired.

Penn glanced at me over his shoulder, and I was sure he noticed that I was lagging behind, but he didn't say anything. He just kept walking, keeping his eyes straight ahead except for when he glanced back every so often to make sure I was still with him.

I was trying to keep up, but I felt a twinge in my side. If I didn't ignore it, Penn would make us go back. I was almost sure of it.

He glanced again, and I forced a smile, but he could tell something was bothering me. I took another step and my leg cramped. When I tried to step down normally, my leg gave out, and I fell down into the snow.

"I'm fine!" I said massaging my calf.

Penn was at my feet in a matter of seconds, crouching down in front of me. He grabbed my foot and pushed the top of it towards my body.

I closed my eyes at the near instant relief. "Just a cramp," I said with a smile even though he must have already figured that out based on his quick response. "It's better now."

"You sure?" he asked, but I could tell he was seconds away from suggesting that we turn back. In fact, when he looked up at the sky, and then back at me, I was sure he was going to.

"I'm positive. Let's go," I said getting onto my feet. My muscle felt tight with the first few steps, almost as though it was bruised, but eventually the feeling subsided.

I was tired, my side was pinching, and my legs were sore, but overall I was fine. And I most definitely wasn't going to give up looking for Carter because of a pulled muscle.

"We're going to have to stop for the day," Penn said with his hands on his hips.

"What? Why? Tons of daylight left," I said.

He held his hand out in front of himself. I watched as the snow fell from the sky and built up on his glove.

"Snow's picking up. Visibility is decreasing," he said as he scanned the area.

"It's not like we're driving a car. You can see far enough."

"For now, but I don't want to get disoriented. I know where to stop around here. Besides, we can check it for signs of Carter," Penn said watching my legs as I took another step. "Come on."

I wasn't sure if I was buying his excuse for wanting to stop. If anyone could navigate their way in some snow, it would be Penn. Surely that was something he'd learned back at HOME's Alaskan base.

I didn't press the issue because maybe he was right. Maybe we would find clues at this place that could lead us to Carter. For all I knew, Carter was there hanging out waiting for the snow to let up.

Then again, it could be something different altogether. Maybe he was there, but he was in trouble. Maybe he needed us. Maybe he was hurt. Injured. Dead.

I vigorously shook the thought from my head and forced myself to walk fast enough so that I could keep up with Penn. It didn't take long for a log cabin to come into view.

Chapter ten.

As we got closer, I saw the cabin wasn't in the best of shape. In fact, it looked as though the roof could collapse at any moment.

"You guys stay here?" I asked scrunching up my nose.

"Yeah, why not?"

"Looks like it could fall down."

Penn shrugged. "Well, it hasn't yet. And it's warmer in there than it is out here."

I followed him towards the house as the surrounding trees thinned out. The cabin wasn't very well hidden.

"It's kind of in the wide open," I said biting at my cheek.

"Kind of, but you'd have to go through a thick forest to get this far. It'll be fine."

Penn pushed the door trying to get it to open, but it seemed as though it was stuck. Or maybe it was locked with someone inside.

He gave it a quick shove with his shoulder, and it squeaked as it jerked across the floor. Perhaps the droopiness of the house had made the door fit tighter in its frame.

"Here we are," Penn said pushing the door just as hard to close it.

The cabin was mostly empty. There was a futon that looked as though it had been chewed up by a wild animal, and spit back out.

Off to the side, was a small bathroom where the door had been ripped off its hinges. The only thing in the room was a toilet.

"Why would someone want to do that?" I asked, gesturing at the missing door.

"Who knows?"

Penn walked into the kitchen area, looking up and down as though he was hoping to find something.

"What are you looking for?"

"Signs that Carter had been here."

I looked at the scummy area on the floor where it looked as though the fridge had also been ripped out. "And?"

"Nothing," he said picking up an old faded wrapper off of the floor.

"What about that?"

"No. Too old," Penn said setting it down on the counter. "I don't think he made it back this far."

I swallowed hard and crossed my arms in front of my body. His words suddenly made me feel colder.

"That doesn't sound good," I said, my voice feeling thick.

Penn didn't respond, which I took to mean that he agreed. He walked back into the living room and looked out of the front window next to the door.

The small cabin only had three windows. One near the bathroom, and two at the front of the building. I wasn't sure if that was a good thing or a bad thing.

"OK, what do we do now?" I said, but I was pretty sure I already knew the answer.

"We wait until morning. Try to get some rest." Penn looked at my legs. "Lots of walking… are you sure you're up for it? We can always go back."

"I'm fine," I said quickly raising my eyebrows at him as I pushed my shoulders back.

I knew he was just concerned about me, but he should have been just as worried about Carter. He was the one we had to worry about.

I'd been through a lot, and I was still standing. Walking through some thick, wet snow with Penn at my side was easy as pie.

"I hope the snow lets up though," I said walking over to the futon, scrunching up my nose as I looked at it. The floor looked as though it might be the better choice of the two.

"It's not so bad. It's more comfortable than it looks." Penn stared out the window, but he must have been able to sense my disgust.

I watched him as his eyes moved side to side as he scanned the area. His face was almost unreadable, but if there was anything to worry about, I'd be able to tell.

I sat down on the futon, keeping my knees together and my body tensed. I was pretty sure a critter of some kind was going to jump out at me at any moment. Maybe even a whole family of them.

"Eat something," Penn said stepping away from his post to make sure the door and all the windows were locked. When he was satisfied the cabin was secured, he sat down next to me and fished out two snack bars and a bottle of water from the backpack.

It would be a few more hours before the sun went down. All I could think about was how we were wasting precious time. We should be out there using every minute we had looking for Carter.

"The snow still coming down?" I asked taking a small bite.

"Yes."

"We should really—"

"First thing in the morning," Penn said stuffing his mouth full, probably because he didn't want to talk about Carter.

I knew he wanted to find him just as badly, the only difference was, he wasn't willing to go out there and risk our lives to do it. Carter could take care of himself. We both knew that, but things could go wrong... I knew that, and I couldn't stop focusing on it.

We spent most of the remaining daylight hours taking turns pacing or staring out the windows. Once all the light was gone, except for the small candle we'd brought with us, Penn lifted the back of the futon and turned it into a slightly lopsided bed.

I squeezed my eyes shut as I lay down on the disgusting cushions, resting as much of my body as possible on Penn.

98

Thankfully, he didn't seem to mind.

He wrapped his arm around me. I must have been more tired than I thought, because that was the last thing I remembered before falling asleep.

* * *

When I opened my eyes, it was still quite dark. Penn was lying next to me with his eyes wide open.

Something had woken me up, and whatever it was had woken Penn too. The second I heard the nearby howl, I realized the noise must have been why we were both awake.

"They're close," he whispered almost inaudibly.

I nodded and held still. As ridiculous as it was, I was afraid to move because they might happen to hear a faint squeak of the rusted futon and know someone was inside the cabin.

After another howl, which sounded closer, Penn slowly got out of bed. I watched as he stealthily made his way over to the window.

I started to rise, but he held his palm up, and I froze in place. His eyes narrowed as he gazed out into the darkness. I assumed he was having trouble seeing in the dark, or maybe it was because of the snow.

He leaned forward and just as he did, something slammed hard into the window. Penn stumbled backward with what almost looked like fear in his eyes, but maybe it had only been shock or surprise. I wasn't sure Penn was capable of showing fear.

When I heard the growl, I knew what had jumped at the window. There was an angry dog-beast outside the cabin, and unfortunately, it already knew we were inside.

Penn straightened his spine and eased his way back to the window. He paused every few steps to look at me.

"Come here," he said waving me over.

I rolled off the bed and walked over to him as quietly as I could. The dog-beast was outside the cabin growling at the wall.

Penn peeked out of the window, and I looked over his shoulder. We both tried to stay back far enough to be out of view. "It looks hungry," I said as I stared at the slim dog-beast that was pacing back and forth in front of the cabin. Every so often it would glance at the window. "And it knows we are in here."

Penn nodded.

"Kill it," I said swallowing down the strange taste in my mouth. I hated having to say the words, but I was afraid of what what happen if it was able to sink its teeth into either one of us.

"Can't. It'll be too loud."

"What are the odds someone is nearby, in the middle of the night in a blizzard?"

Penn shook his head. "Probably slim, but we can't risk it. HOME was just here not that long ago. Maybe they never left. Maybe they came back."

I knew he was right, but I wanted that thing gone. "Maybe he'll leave," I said with a shrug.

"Yeah, maybe," Penn said, but I knew he didn't believe it would. If the dog-beast was starving, it wasn't going to give up that easily. "But animals do crazy things when they are desperate."

It was my turn to nod. People did crazy things when they were desperate too.

"We'll give it some time… see what it does," Penn said as he stared at the dog-beast. I could tell when his eyes shifted out in another direction that he was worried about the dog-beast calling out for his friends. "A very short while."

After five minutes or so, the dog-beast sat down near the door. It breathed heavily while keeping its angry eyes glued to it. The only time it looked away from the door was to glance at the window to see if we were still there.

"OK. We are just going to sit down and see if it'll leave. If it doesn't see or hear us, maybe it'll give up, although I really doubt it," Penn said leading me back to the gross futon.

We sat down at the same time, and when the futon creaked, we both paused and looked at one another. When the dog-beast didn't react, we put down the rest of our weight.

I stared at my hands, trying to listen through the wall, but I couldn't hear anything. Somehow though, I knew it was still out there.

Just when I started to relax my clenched fists, the dog-beast jumped into the door. The entire door made a loud cracking noise before rattling to a stop. I let out a small squeak as I jumped off of the futon.

My shaking hand covered my mouth as I pulled out my gun.

The door had been stuck in the frame, but the panels that made up the door were far weaker than I had realized. It wouldn't hold up if the dog-beast kept throwing itself into it. When the dog jumped into the door again, I knew we had to do something. We couldn't let it get inside.

I pointed my gun at the still-shaking door. If Penn wouldn't take the dog-beast out... I would.

Chapter eleven.

Penn took a giant step and pushed on my arm until the gun was aimed down at the floor. His eyes were wide, pleading with me not to pull the trigger.

"It's howling could draw other dog-beasts, or even HOME if they are out there," I said feeling the tension around my brows. "We have to do something. It's not going to leave on its own."

I could tell by the way Penn was looking at me that he'd already considered all that. He was still trying to figure out how to handle the situation.

I stepped away from Penn and started pacing. He watched me moving, keeping his eyes mostly focused on my hand that was still holding the gun.

"OK!" Penn said in a hard whisper, waving his hand to get me to stop moving. "OK."

He rubbed his forehead vigorously

with his fingertips. It was obvious he was having a little trouble coming up with a plan, which had me a little worried. Penn always knew the right thing to do.

"Can you snap its necks?" I asked.

Penn narrowed his eyes and cocked his head to the side.

"When Nora and I were leaving the facility to find you, she just straddled one of them and snapped its neck with ease. It looked like she'd done it a million times. Did they teach that at HOME?" I asked.

"Um, no," he said looking at me as if he wasn't sure if I was remembering what happened correctly. "At least it wasn't something they taught when I was there."

The look on his face shifted, and it seemed as though he was thinking over what I'd told him. When he started to rub his palms together, I knew he was considering making an attempt, but if he didn't know what he was doing, it would be far too risky.

"OK, something else then," I said, but I could tell it was too late. His mind was already putting together a plan.

Penn grinned, and his confidence returned. "I can do it. OK. Yeah."

The dog-beast threw itself into the door again, and I wasn't sure I had time to talk him out of whatever his plan was. Then it was quiet. The dog-beast stopped, and I wondered if it had actually decided to give up, but then it threw itself against the window.

It let out a sharp squeal as though it had hurt itself and went back to the door. Thankfully, it seemed to have given up on the window, because I didn't think it would have taken more than two or three attempts to break it.

"OK when it jumps again, I want you to open the door," Penn said tapping his palm with his fingertip.

"That sounds like a terrible idea," I said shaking my head. If we were just going to let it inside, I might as well just stick my arm out the door and let it have a snack.

"No… no, it'll work. I'll jump on it and catch it in that blanket."

"That blanket is a rag with an excessive amount of holes."

"I can do this," Penn said puffing out his chest.

If the dog-beast kept jumping at the door, eventually it would get inside anyway. It would probably be better to attempt Penn's plan and keep the door intact for the rest of the night. Otherwise, more dog-beast would probably find their way in, as there wouldn't be anything to keep them outside and us safe.

The dog-beast let out a sharp howl that pierced my brain. I pressed my hands over my ears until it stopped.

It was getting ever more desperate. And I could tell by the frequent growling that it was getting more angry too.

When the dog-beast threw itself into the door, Penn ran to the window. "OK when I tell you, open the door. Timing is very important."

"Oh crap, like—"

"Now!" Penn shouted and readied himself with the blanket spread out in front of him.

I quickly pulled open the door, and the dog-beast flopped awkwardly inside the room. It was as though it had expected to hit the door, and when it hadn't, it had become confused.

Penn leaped towards the dog-beast and landed right on top of it. The blanket was so thin I was worried that its snapping mouth was going to make contact with Penn's arm.

The dog-beast was far stronger than Penn had been ready for and it swiftly wiggled itself free. It jumped sideways towards the kitchen and away from Penn. The look on its face was sheer anger, and its eyes showed it desperation.

"Shit!" Penn shouted as he tried to ready the blanket again.

"Now what?" I screeched, wishing Penn would just take out his gun and end the situation.

The dog-beast jumped away from Penn every time he tried to get closer. It almost seemed as though it had one eye on me and the other on Penn.

It hopped around the room, jumping away from the wall and then onto the futon, making its way closer and closer to me.

I took several massive steps back, moving in the opposite direction of each one of the beast's hops. All it really had to do was launch itself at me, and it would probably be able to get to my throat before Penn could do anything to stop it.

Saliva dripping from its mouth as it let out a low growl. It leaned back, sticking its backside into the air. I was pretty sure it realized what it should do. If it wasn't going to survive, it was going to take me out with it.

The dog-beast bared its teeth. I could

tell by the darkness in its beady eyes that all it was thinking about was sinking its teeth into me.

"Can you get it?" I said wanting to aim my gun, but afraid the dog-beast would react before I could pull the trigger.

"I think so," Penn said, but his voice was rough and unconvincing.

"If you don't get it soon, I'm going to shoot it."

"Don't. I got it."

Penn stepped left and then right, trying to corner the dog-beast, but it waited for just the right moment before launching itself in my direction. Penn lost his footing slightly and slipped as the dog-beast managed to get past him.

I dodged to the side, narrowly missing the dog-beast's jaw clamping down on my leg. My body slammed into the wall so hard even my teeth rattled from the jolt.

The dog-beast slid to a stop and tried to ready itself for another attack. Penn twisted and jumped, managing to wrap the dog-beast up inside the old blanket before it could do anything.

Once he had control, he didn't hesitate. Penn's arms moved fast as he cranked its neck to the side, and in an instant, the dog-beast was lying there lifeless.

I pressed my hands against my chest, trying to coax my breathing into returning to normal. I didn't even want to think about how close I had been to being bitten.

HOME had a cure, but there would be no way I'd get it. If the dog-beast had gotten me, Penn would have had to take me out, and I wasn't sure if he would have been able to.

Penn wrapped the blanket tightly around the dead dog-beast and dragged it out of the cabin. I leaned forward with my hands on my knees, worried I wasn't going to be able to calm down.

It had only taken Penn a few minutes to move the dog-beast's body before he was back inside the cabin. He didn't bother to bury it, there just wasn't time. If anyone came by and saw the blanket lying outside, it would have been a pretty big clue that someone was inside the cabin.

"I covered it with snow," Penn said closing and locking the door. It was as though he could read my mind.

"Good," I said making my way over to the futon, so I could sit down. I leaned forward and put my head between my knees.

"Are you OK?"

"Yeah… mostly," I said between sharp breaths. It felt as though I had run a marathon.

I couldn't believe that the dog-beast had been inside the cabin, jumping around, almost getting me. Its putrid scent of damp, dirty socks that had sat out too long still lingered inside the small building.

Penn walked past me and over to the window. He stared outside as though he was expecting the dog-beast to come back to life, or maybe he was anticipating more of them coming, looking for their fallen comrade.

"We'll have to take turns sleeping," Penn said. My whole body jerked at the sound of his voice. I hadn't been expecting him to say anything, and it had startled me. "You sleep first. We'll need as much rest as we can get for tomorrow."

"But—"

"No. Just do it," Penn said without looking at me.

I knew it was pointless to argue. This wasn't an argument I could win. And even though I didn't want to admit it, I knew he was right.

We would need as much sleep as we could get, and because of the encounter with the dog-beast, we were already going to be short on it. Even though it would be hard, I had to do it for Carter.

I smiled and nodded. "OK. Wake me in a couple hours. You'll need some sleep too."

"Sure."

I curled up and closed my eyes. It was the first time we had to take turns keeping watch in quite a while, and I didn't like it. It felt as though we were taking steps back instead of forward to the peaceful life we'd hoped to have.

I wasn't even sure we could find that peace until we had Carter back. We had to find him. We just had to.

Chapter twelve.

The next day it was still snowing, but not quite as bad as it had been. The air outside of the cabin was crisp, and it helped wake me up, even though I was tired as hell.

I was more determined than ever to find Carter. After what had happened with the dog-beast, I couldn't help but wonder if maybe he had his own confrontation.

I followed Penn down the way they'd always taken to town for their runs. Even though I was utterly clueless as to where we were going, or even what direction we were headed, I could tell Penn knew exactly where he was.

We had walked several miles, and I was already doing everything I could to convince myself that my legs weren't tired. They didn't get the option to be tired when Carter was out there possibly in trouble.

My eyes scanned the horizon between the falling snowflakes, but all I could see was tree trunks and the white, snow-covered ground. It was just a mish-mash of grays, browns, and white that seemed to go on for miles and miles.

"It's quiet," I murmured, and it sounded too loud in the stillness of our surroundings.

"Indeed," Penn said. He held his head still, but I knew his eyes were moving around methodically and his ears were probably listening to sounds at abnormally far distances.

Penn's super powers were definitely in the ON position which, really, they had been in most of the time. Although, there were a few times back at our place where he'd had them off, which was hopefully a good thing.

When we were alone, it had just been the real Penn and me. I absolutely loved that side of him, but if it hadn't been for the HOME training instilled in his brain, I probably wouldn't still be alive.

Penn's head cocked to the side sharply.

"What's that?" I said squinting at something in the distance. It was a different color than everything else we'd seen for the last several miles. Whatever it was, stood out like a sore thumb. Although I couldn't tell what it was, it appeared to be swinging from a tree branch. "Do you see that?"

"I do," Penn said as he quickened his pace. I moved my feet faster to keep up as my pulse raced.

I wasn't sure what it was, but something about it didn't feel right. There was suddenly an awful taste in my throat that I couldn't swallow down.

When we got closer, I recognized something about what I was seeing. The color. That bright, orange-brown was the same color as Carter's jacket.

"Penn," I said, my voice shaking. He looked at me, but I didn't know what to say. I wasn't even sure what I was looking at. My lips felt as though they were stuck together.

I moved my head side to side and tried to make sense of what I was seeing. It was Carter's jacket, but it was moving back and forth, swaying in the slight breeze.

Penn was standing slightly in front of me, and I could see his shoulders moving up and down. Did he know what was going on? Did he understand?

I started to run towards Carter's jacket, but Penn grabbed my arm. When I met his eyes, I saw something… something I didn't like.

"What's going on?" I said turning back.

"Slow down." Penn's eyes were squinted, and his lips were pressed tightly together. "Take it easy."

Penn grabbed my arm and led us closer. It didn't take more than a few steps for me to realize that Carter was still inside the jacket that was hanging from the tree branch.

I'd seen the legs dangling, but it was like my brain wouldn't put the pieces together until I moved closer. Maybe it had been attempting to save me from whatever had happened.

"Carter!" I called out, but he didn't look up at us. I could feel the cold wetness stinging my eyes as I turned to look at Penn. "Why isn't he answering? What's going on?"

"I'm not sure."

"Is he dead?"

Penn just shook his head. "We have to be careful. Whoever put him up there could still be around."

"I don't understand," I said with a sharp gasp. I was doing everything I could to fight back the emotions that were threatening to burst forwards and overtake me. Seeing Carter was overwhelming, but seeing him hanging from the tree was unexpected. I couldn't make sense of what I was seeing or what I was feeling.

Each breath I took stabbed my lungs. We had to get him down. We had to save him... if saving him was still an option.

"Who did this to him? HOME? Those men? Why?" I asked, my words raspy and awkward. They hadn't even sounded like they'd come out of my mouth.

"Not sure, but it doesn't really seem like something HOME would do, does it?" Penn was still looking around more than he was looking at poor Carter.

"No," I said, punctuating my sentence with another weird gasp that I was sure Penn noticed.

I wanted to go to him, but Penn was still holding me. He was being extra cautious.

"Penn," I said trying to pull my arm away.

"No."

"Please, let me check on him," I said taking a sharp breath.

"Ros, shh! It could be some kind of

trap."

Penn took each step carefully as if he was afraid a trap would spring and we'd be pulled up into the tree. But nothing like that happened. It was so calm and quiet, it didn't even seem possible that anyone could be around.

As we got closer to the tree something happened. Carter's leg's twitched. He was alive.

Chapter thirteen.

When we got within ten feet of him, Penn held me back as he looked around carefully. After a few seconds, he let go of me. He must have been satisfied that we weren't stepping into a trap.

"Carter," Penn said softly as he walked closer. Carter didn't move, but I could see his body was swaying ever so slightly with his very shallow breaths. "Carter!"

"We have to get him down," I said stepping even closer. I touched his foot slightly as I looked up to see how he was attached to the tree.

When I saw his face, I almost lost it. The handsome face I'd known so well, looked beaten and bruised. His face was swollen, and there was dried blood on his cheeks and around his mouth. I wasn't sure if his eyes were closed because he couldn't open them, or if he was unconscious.

"What happened to you, Carter?" I whispered not expecting an answer.

Carter's eyes popped open and his mouth twisted to the side awkwardly. I stumbled backward, and his eyes followed me at the same time his arms reached out for me.

The rope around his neck pulled tighter, and he whined. Carter put his hands to his neck as his body stiffened in an attempt to settle himself, but at the same time, I knew he wanted to get his hands on me.

He had a crazed, aggressive look in his eyes I'd seen before. I knew what had happened to Carter, although I didn't know why he was hanging from a tree. Carter had been bitten by a dog-beast.

"Dammit!" I yelled as I dropped to my knees. We were too late. There wasn't anything we could do for him. I slammed my fists so hard into the snow my arms tingled.

Penn must have realized as well because he didn't say anything. He could tell just as well as I could that Carter was no longer in Carter's body.

"No, no, no, no!" I said, each word louder than the last. Penn stepped over to

120

help me up, but I knew what he really wanted to do was keep me quiet.

"I'm so sorry," he said avoiding looking at Carter. His eyes were wet, but he was focused on me.

"Look at him! We have to get him down," I said taking a step forward again as though I'd forgotten what had happened. When he growled, and the saliva dripped out of the side of his mouth, I remembered.

I let out a whimper which turned into a shoulder-shaking cry. I pressed my face hard into my hands as the gravity of the situation fully sunk in.

It was over. There was truly no way Penn and I could survive. HOME won.

Their dog-beasts took out those they couldn't get to. I let my hands fall from my face. My sadness changed into anger so fast it made my stomach turn, and I wasn't sure if I'd be able to hold the minimal contents down.

"Why would HOME do this?" I asked, but Penn just shook his head.

"I don't think they did."

"Then who did?"

Penn lightly shrugged his shoulders as he looked around the area again. His eyes shifted downward when he circled back around to Carter.

"Well, he didn't climb up there himself." I almost wanted to take my words back, because if it had been Penn, he probably would have found a way to get himself up there, to protect me from what he'd become. "At least I don't think so."

"No, he probably didn't," Penn said, glancing at Carter briefly. "He's been up there awhile. I don't think he has much time left."

"There's nothing we can do for him anyway. He's gone."

Penn kicked the snow. I didn't even want to know what he was thinking we should do.

Carter let out another growl as he swung himself towards us. When he couldn't reach either of us, he howled like a wild animal in pain as he looked towards the sky.

Carter's nostrils flared like a bull, and he put his arm to his mouth. He opened wide as he tried to chew through his own jacket to get to his arm. I could tell by the tears and hanging threads on his sleeves that this hadn't been the first time he'd attempted to get to his arms.

Penn's mouth dropped open, and I

saw his fingers twitch. Carter's actions were affecting him. He couldn't stand to see what was happening to his friend, someone he'd grown quite close to. His switch wasn't entirely flipped, he was allowing himself to feel, and I knew that meant he was off his guard.

"Penn," I said gently, trying to break through his thoughts.

There was a long pause, but he looked away from Carter and focused his attention on me. After a few seconds, it looked as though the spell he had been under had been broken. He knew enough not to look back at Carter.

I didn't want to admit it, I wanted to have hope, but deep down I knew we couldn't save him. Carter was gone. The poison from the dog-beast bite had taken him from us.

Only HOME could save him with their cure, but that wouldn't happen. And I thought it was quite possible he was too far gone to even be cured.

"We just can't leave him up there," I said looking away when the rope tightened a bit more as he struggled against it. Eventually, he'd choke to death. Whoever put him up there hadn't done a good job, or maybe they had done exactly what they had intended to do.

"I know."

"We can't take him down like this," I said, but that was probably quite obvious to Penn.

He closed his eyes for a second and slowly opened them again. He sighed. "I know."

Penn stepped closer to me, and I wished I could take away his pain. This wasn't like Penn at all. He was letting his emotions get to him, which made me a little nervous…because if something happened, I wasn't sure he'd be ready.

I opened my mouth to say something, although I wasn't exactly sure what, but I didn't get a chance. Penn pulled me into his arms and buried his face into my neck.

Less than a minute passed before he took a deep breath and pulled his gun out from his waistband. Neither of us watched, but the second I heard the loud pop of the gun, there wasn't a damn thing I could do to stop the tears from rolling down my cheeks.

Out of the corner of my eye, I could see Carter's limp body swinging slightly back and forth. I took a deep breath and bit my lip as I stepped away from Penn.

"We have to work fast," he said, and I followed him closely as we moved to Carter's body. "It was too loud, but I didn't have a choice. Someone could come."

Penn sounded as though he was pleading his case to me as to why he had to pull the trigger. It was like he thought I'd blame him if someone came looking for whoever had shot the gun.

"I know."

Penn started climbing the tree, easing his way across the top of the branch to the rope that was holding Carter. He pulled out a pocket knife and started sawing at the rope.

"Come on," he said to himself, or to the knife. He raised his head for a second and looked around, but there wasn't anyone in the area.

After a few more minutes, Carter's body dropped hard to the ground. His blood stood out as it started to stain the once perfectly white snow.

"There's no time. We'll just cover him," Penn said dragging him behind a large tree.

"Can we take him back to the house… bury him properly?" I said biting my lip.

"No." Penn looked at me as though I'd lost my mind. "He's far too heavy. It would take us too long."

I nodded.

"Maybe we can come back another time. Do this right," I said, but Penn didn't respond.

Penn started scooping up snow and packing it down on top of Carter. As soon as spring came, if it ever came, the snow would melt, and he'd still be here. That was if the dog-beasts didn't get to him first.

I pushed the thought out of my mind and started helping Penn cover him. We made it as thick as we could, but Penn was nervous we were taking too long. He looked up at our surroundings more than he looked at what his hands were doing.

"Let's go," Penn said grabbing me by the arm and leading me away.

I wondered if he could tell I was having trouble leaving Carter. My feet felt heavy. It just didn't feel right. I was getting awfully sick of having to leave people behind.

Who would be next... Penn? Me?

I knew by the direction we were walking, Penn was taking me back to our place. There wasn't anywhere else for us to go, or anything for us to do but to go back.

"If you go on another run, this could happen to you," I said. When the tears didn't pour out of my eyes, I was almost surprised, but then again, maybe there just weren't any tears left. "You'll go out one day, and you won't come back because you're out here hanging in a tree. Then what will I do?"

I swallowed hard. There was a pinching feeling in my chest. It was almost as though I could already feel my heart breaking at the loss of Penn.

He didn't say anything. He was supposed to tell me that he'd never leave me, that he wouldn't go on any runs because he didn't want to lose me either, but he didn't.

I gritted my teeth wanting to scream at him. But of course, I didn't. I held it all in just like always. He was aware of the risks, I just had to hope it would sink in.

There wasn't much that would stop Penn from going on a run if he believed it was the right thing to do. If we needed something to stay alive. But we didn't, we had food, we had water... what else could we absolutely need that we didn't already have enough of in our basement?

Hopefully, we had it all. The way it was, our basement had things that anyone still alive, except those at HOME, would consider a luxury. But would Penn ever feel that way? Probably not.

Even though I didn't feel like discussing it, I opened my mouth, but I couldn't find the words I wanted. I turned to Penn who looked back at me with wide, solemn eyes.

He tapped his lips twice with his index finger and started to lead us in another direction. I didn't say anything, but I knew by the look on his face that something was wrong.

I looked over my shoulder, but I didn't see anything, nor did I hear anything unusual. All I heard was the crackle of the trees and the crunch of the snow each time we took a step.

When I looked straight ahead, Penn was gone.

Chapter fourteen.

I wanted to call out for him, but this wasn't the first time Penn had vanished. In fact, since he had disappeared, I was pretty sure something must be going on… something I was completely oblivious to.

My faith was resting on the fact that Penn knew what he was doing. And if he was wrong, maybe it was just our time to be done in this world.

I kept walking forward, trying not to let my nerves and anxiety overtake me. It would have been easy to just turn around, put my hands up and call it a day. If it was my time, then so be it.

As I kept walking in the new direction, the one that I was sure was leading away from our home, I heard noises. Someone was walking behind me, and it wasn't Penn.

Whoever it was tried to be quiet but they were failing miserably. Not only could

I hear each footstep, I could hear their breathing as they got closer and closer.

Even though my heart started to pound, I kept walking, trying hard not to alter my speed. Whoever was behind me was increasing theirs and gaining on me, but I didn't want to give away that I knew I was being followed.

Dammit, Penn.

Where was he? What was taking so long?

I wasn't going to be able to maintain a calm pace much longer. The person behind me was probably wondering what had happened to my traveling companion if he'd seen him. My nerves were about to get the better of me when I heard a grunt close behind me.

When I turned around, I saw Penn on top of a man. I let out a sharp gasp when he pressed his gun against the man's chin.

"Why are you following us?" Penn said practically spitting in the man's face.

The man stared up at him with wide eyes and mumbled something I couldn't make out. It looked as though he was afraid to move his jaw too much with the gun held up against it.

Penn eased up slightly, and the man's

lip quivered. "I didn't mean any harm," he said with a gulp. "Just looking for my friend. He headed west and hasn't returned, have you seen him?"

"Aw, come now, you don't really think I'll fall for that do you?" Penn said shaking his head and clicking his tongue. He pointed briefly at the surroundings with the barrel of his gun. "We're in the middle of nowhere, you surely know things have changed, and you're walking behind us, stalking us more likely. Maybe you were just going to walk up and introduce yourself. Shake our hands. Were you going to invite us over for dinner?"

I could tell Penn was getting angrier with each word. His emotions over Carter were evident. Penn wanted to take it out on someone.

The man's hands twitched every so often, but it wasn't the jerking that I noticed, it was what he had on his hands that caught my attention. He was wearing Carter's gloves.

"Where did you get those?" I asked the man. He turned his head and looked at me for a moment before turning back to Penn. "Those aren't your gloves."

"I found them," the man said looking

at Penn as though he had asked the question.

Penn laughed. "Really? Where?"

"On the ground," the man said, but the words came out more like a question, as though he was hoping we'd believe it. I didn't need Penn's super ninja HOME training to know the man was lying through his brown-stained teeth.

I stepped closer so I could watch the man's reaction. "No. You found them on our friend," I said. "Did you put him up in the tree?"

"What tree?" the man answered quickly.

Penn squeezed his lips together hard before he blew out a sharp breath. "You better start talking, or I swear I'll pull the trigger."

"You're going to do that either way!" the man said practically sobbing.

Penn shrugged, and the man let out a soft, agonized whimper.

"Your odds are better if you start talking," I said, but it wasn't true. I was pretty sure we all were well aware of what Penn would do after he was done asking questions.

"Are they?" the man said making a noise akin to a chuckle. "Of course they ain't."

"Why did you put him in the tree?" Penn asked.

The man swallowed hard and tightened the muscles in his face as though he was preparing himself for the bullet. But then his face relaxed. "I found him. He'd already been bitten. He begged me to kill him," the man sniffed, "but I couldn't do it."

"And then he told you to take his gloves?" I asked crossing my arms.

It didn't seem to me that the bearded man lying on the ground who looked as though he didn't eat very often, would be able to get Carter into a tree by himself. Carter was strong, and if he'd been bitten, would he have just allowed the man to do it? Somehow I didn't think so.

"How did you get him up in the tree by yourself?" Penn asked. I could tell he wasn't buying it either.

"I just rigged it up. Used some rope and pulled him up there. It was what he wanted," the man said with wide eyes. "I didn't want to. I wanted to try to help him."

"I bet you did," Penn said.

Penn glanced at me for a second. He wanted to know what I was thinking, and I was pretty sure the look on my face showed him exactly what he wanted to see…that I didn't believe a single word out of the guy's mouth.

As I moved my head ever so slightly to nod, someone cried out in the distance. I sharply turned my head to look at Penn.

"Help me!" the far-away voice shouted. It was faint, but it was clear.

The man quickly shifted his weight and flipped Penn off-balance. He wiggled free, got to his feet and started to run away.

Penn tried to aim a shot, but the man was weaving quickly in and out of the trees. It seemed as though he knew the area very well with how precise his maneuvers were.

"At least try!" I shouted, but Penn lowered his gun. It was too late.

He tipped his head towards the ground. "Arrrrgh!" he shouted, looking at his gun as if it had been to blame.

"He's getting," I said looking back out to the trees. "Away."

The man was gone. Penn started to walk over to the path of footprints the man had left in the snow. I couldn't help but think the reason he wasn't going after the man was because I was with him.

I stood next to him and tried to make eye contact, but Penn wouldn't look up.

The expression he was wearing was one I'd see before. Penn was frustrated and disappointed with himself.

"I'm too afraid that HOME is always waiting in the wings to take me away from you," he said softly.

I nodded. I could understand how he felt, but at the same time, I didn't want the guy who was probably responsible for Carter's death to escape justice.

Penn and I both looked away when we heard that same voice calling for help again. Penn looked at the path of footprints and then in the direction of the voice.

"They're quite loud," I murmured. "They're going to draw attention."

"Let's check it out," Penn said.

"Are you sure?" I asked. The curiosity in Penn's eyes was unmistakable. He wanted answers, and maybe the shouting voice would give us some.

We could follow the footprints to see where they'd take us, but there was always a chance we'd walk right into an ambush. Or we could check out who was calling for help…which could also lead us right into an ambush.

"Maybe we should just go back home. Nothing will bring him back," I said with a hard sniff.

"We'll check it out and then go back," Penn said.

"It could be a trap," I said even though I knew Penn was well aware of that.

"We'll be careful."

We started trying to follow the voice, but there was so much delay between each call for help. One thing I was sure of was that he wasn't too far away.

"Please! Oh, please God, help me!" the voice said. And this time, when it wasn't a shout, I knew we were even closer.

I pointed out towards a small grouping of trees and Penn nodded. We took maybe twenty steps before we saw the owner of the voice.

Chapter fifteen.

I looked at Penn, and could tell we both knew it was another victim of the man that got away. The guy hanging in this tree wasn't as far gone as Carter had been. He was still well aware of what was going on around him.

We approached carefully, but when I stepped on a twig, and it made a small cracking noise, the man in the tree looked our way.

"Hello? Who's there?" he asked cautiously. I couldn't tell if he sounded happy to know someone was out there, or if he was frightened that something else was going to happen to him.

Penn looked around carefully before gesturing for me to follow. We slowly approached the man in the tree.

"Oh, thank God," he said almost in tears. "My name is Terry McLaine, and I was just out looking for supplies when I was attacked. Please, I need your help."

The man's eyes were filled with fear. I could tell he wasn't absolutely sure if he should trust us, but it also seemed as though he believed he was out of options.

"How did you get up in that tree?" Penn asked.

"I was knocked out. When I came to, I was up here." The man, Terry, reached out as though he was begging for help, and that's when I saw it.

On his arm was a big, red, pus-filled wound. He, too, had been bitten.

"That's when I started calling for help, just minutes ago," Terry looked at us suspiciously. "You sure did get here fast."

Penn looked at me and then back at the man. "Looks like you're hurt. How did that happen?"

The man looked down at his arm and squinted at the wound. "I… I don't know. I… I don't remember."

"What was it you were doing out here again? Looking for supplies, you said?" Penn asked as he stroked his chin.

"Yes, and then I was attacked. Please, you have to help me down."

Penn looked at me, and I bit my lip. For all I knew, the man was telling the truth, but he'd been bitten, our options were limited.

"I don't think I can do that," Penn said as he started walking around the man hanging from the tree. His expression was blank, unreadable. "Take off your jacket."

"What? No! Why would I do that? It's too cold out here," Terry said choking slightly when he tried to cross his arms. Penn was positioned behind the man, so Terry kept his eyes on me.

At first it seemed like a strange request, but after a second I knew what had crossed Penn's mind. He wanted to make sure good ol' Terry wasn't from HOME.

"Take it off," I said clasping my wrist with my free hand. I rested my hands against the front of my body, making sure the man saw the gun.

"Shit. How the hell am I supposed to take off my jacket while hanging from this damn tree? If I move too fast, the rope starts tightening. I'll be strangled," he said, but the look in his eyes had changed. While he still looked terrified, it also seemed as though part of him knew what we were looking for.

"Carefully," I said with a smirk.

The man started to raise his arm, but

the rope tightened just as he said it would. Terry pulled at the rope around his neck, trying to loosen it. After a few seconds, he forced himself to relax and, although the rope was tighter, he seemed to be OK.

"It's not going to work," Terry said with a heavy sigh. "But, yes, OK, I know why you're asking."

"Do you?" Penn said taking a step closer to the man. His gun was pointed at him, but I wasn't sure if Terry was aware of it or not.

"Yes. You want to know if I have a tattoo," Terry said swallowing hard. "I do, but please, don't kill me. I don't want to die."

Penn's jaw was clenched so hard I could see the veins and tendons in his neck pushing against his skin. "No one does, Terry. But lots of people have."

"No one should die like this," Terry said.

My thoughts went straight to Carter. The man was right, no one should have to die like that.

"You help us, we'll help you. Sound fair, Ter?" Penn said.

"I'll try, but I'm not sure I have whatever it is you're looking for." Terry tried to turn to look at Penn, but the rope around his neck didn't allow the movement.

"What do you do for HOME?" Penn asked.

"Resource collector."

Penn shook his head side to side to indicate to me that he didn't believe him. I could see Terry's eyes, but they weren't helping me determine whether he was being honest or not.

"Just you? No vehicle?"

"I got separated from my team. The medical team."

"Medical?" I asked cocking my head to the side. "Out here? In the middle of nowhere?"

Terry nodded. "We check everything from the big cities to old, barely standing houses."

"Where is the rest of your team?" Penn asked.

"Um, I'm not sure."

"Wrong answer, Terry," Penn said and pointed his gun at the back of Terry's skull.

The man started waving his hands ever so slightly, his eyes bulging. He was looking at me as though he hoped I'd do something to help him.

"I was searching a house, maybe I had

the meet-up time wrong, I don't know, but when I got back they were gone," Terry said speaking fast. "Although," Terry said with a weak chuckle, "I suspect they did it on purpose, but that's neither here nor there."

Penn widened his stance and tilted his head slightly as he narrowed his eyes. He was lining up his shot.

"Some men, HOME, were out here dressed in uniform, surveying the land, what was the purpose of all that?" Penn asked. It looked as though he was prepared for another wrong answer.

"I don't know much, but we're expanding. Building lookout towers. I'd imagine they were looking for a suitable location, but that isn't knowledge I'm privy to," Terry said. His face didn't give away a single clue whether or not he was telling the truth.

It did seem to make sense with what we'd overheard, but this was HOME, nothing they said could be believed. At least not as far as I was concerned.

"Why lookout towers?" Penn asked.

The man winced as he scratched at his arm. "Oh, Jesus," he murmured as he looked at the wound on his arm more closely. "You can kill me, just don't let me die up here like this. I can feel it spreading through my veins now."

I nodded at the man because I didn't want to give him false hope. He was probably going to be taken over soon. The bite was huge, and the poison was probably spreading fast. But whether he died up in the tree, or down on the ground would be up to Penn.

"The towers?" I said tapping my foot into the snow.

"I don't know exactly. Lookout towers, watching for strays. Just to keep our land safe," Terry said. I couldn't be sure, but it seemed as though he was telling the truth. He really didn't know anything more about the towers than we did.

Terry's eyes darted out towards the horizon. I quickly looked over my shoulder to see if I could tell what he was looking at. I could sense my sharp movement had made Penn nervous.

He looked around, shifting his gun this way and that, but he didn't see anything out of the ordinary. Maybe the guy wasn't looking for help, maybe he was planning his escape. If we helped him down, and he got away, maybe his plan was to try to make it back to HOME for the antidote.

Terry looked into my eyes. "It won't be long before HOME controls everything. You both should really just give up."

"No," I said shaking my head before he even finished his sentence. Not in a million years would I surrender to HOME.

"Please, that's all I know, just help me down," Terry said shifting his eyes away again.

I crossed my arms in front of my chest and looked up at Terry. I didn't want him to have to die in the tree either, but I wasn't sure if there was any way around it.

"Is there anything else you can, or will, tell us about HOME?" I asked pushing my shoulders back.

"That's all I know. My job is to gather medicine, which I probably won't be allowed to do again. Whoever—"

The loud pop of Penn's gun cut the man off. His head dropped down, and his body slowly swayed back and forth just as Carter's had.

I quickly looked away, and before I knew it, Penn was at my side pulling me along. He was in such a hurry... our pace was almost at a run. Penn wanted to get us out of there as fast as he possibly could.

"You could have just left him up

there," I said, my stomach twisting into a tight knot.

"I didn't have a choice," Penn said pulling me along. "I was going to do it even before I knew about the HOME tattoo."

I wasn't sure if there was anyone Penn would let live. At least not anymore. After everything we'd been through, he wasn't about to take any risks.

I wasn't exactly sure how I should feel about any of it. Of course I understood, but at the same time, there were probably still good people left in the world. After all, it wasn't that long ago we'd found Carter and Alice at the side of the road, and they were just as good as any of us had been.

Maybe there were still others like us out there too. But we wouldn't ever know because Penn would keep pulling that trigger before we could find out.

I had thought Nora was good, but that hadn't turned out well. Maybe I should have a heart as cold as Penn's, but I didn't think that was possible for me.

My heart was significantly colder than ever before, but still, there was a touch of warmth that would always remain. I couldn't help it. It was just who I was.

The only thing that could extinguish

that tiny bit of warmth I had left would be if something happened to Penn.

I looked up at the darkening sky. It was hard to believe that so much time had passed. We hadn't even had much of a chance to eat, or drink and soon it would be dark.

"Are we going to travel through the night?" I asked having vivid flashbacks of the last time I traveled through the area at night. I'd fallen into a trap and almost died.

"No," Penn said walking fast as he looked around. It appeared as though he was looking for something specific.

We walked for maybe ten more minutes before he nodded and stopped in front of a large tree with thick roots. I scrunched up my nose as I looked around, unsure why we weren't moving anymore.

"Why are we stopping?" I asked breathing heavily.

"This is where we're staying for the night," Penn said, gesturing towards the tree.

"Um, there's nothing here."

Penn crouched down and dug out some dirt below a large root that had broken through the surface. "Go on, get inside."

"Huh?" I asked looking at him as

though he'd lost his mind. All I could see was thick roots covered with snow. Yet, he was smiling as though he'd revealed something amazing.

"Like this," Penn said lowering his body to the ground and sliding under the big root.

I got down on the ground and took a deep breath as I stared into the darkness. It seemed insane, but I followed him under the tree.

Chapter sixteen.

I kept moving downward until I realized I could sit up. At some point in the past, Penn must have dug out the area to have a little hiding space under the tree in case of emergencies.

I was pretty sure no one would ever be able to see us under the tree. It was cold, but the giant tree blocked most of the wind, keeping it tolerable.

"You have all sorts of little surprises up your sleeves, don't you?" I said with a small smile.

"I do," he said grinning back. "But I have some bad news."

"Oh?"

Penn scooted closer to me. "We can't have a fire under here… gets too smoky and it would be kind of a fire hazard. It's going to get really dark down here when all the sunlight is gone."

"Oh," I said unable to keep the disappointment out of my voice. We wouldn't be able to see anything, but hopefully, nothing could see us either. "What if a dog-beast gets in here?"

"They won't," Penn said pushing our packs in front of the little opening we'd crawled through. "This little place is quite safe. No one could find it unless they knew exactly where to look and only two people knew where it was."

"You and Carter?"

Penn nodded. He turned his head to the side so I wouldn't see the pain in his eyes.

"And now you too," he said.

"Oh, don't count me. I'd never be able to find this place again no matter how hard I tried."

I smiled, but Penn was lost in his thoughts. Likely on Carter.

Penn and Carter had grown quite close. They had spent a lot of time with one another while working to make our place safer.

I took his hand into mine, but I couldn't say anything. It wasn't like Penn would want to talk about it, and I didn't really want to talk about it either. Losing people was just something I had to deal with. It was part of this life whether we liked it or not.

The only thing left in my mind was "who would be next?" And that was something I definitely didn't want to talk about.

"You should try to get some rest," Penn said leaning back against the dirt wall. After two seconds he quickly jerked forward and opened his pack. "It's going to get colder." Penn unfolded a thin silver blanket that had a shiny foil-like appearance. He tucked his backpack into place and leaned back again.

"What's that?"

"A thermal blanket. Found it on a run once."

He rested back and pulled me into his arm before carefully spreading the blanket over both of us as best as he could. We snuggled close together, and I rested my head against his shoulder.

"I know this is really awkward timing considering everything, but I have to tell you something," Penn said sucking in a deep breath. "I have to tell you now."

"What is it?" I said without looking at him. I didn't know if I should feel scared, but whatever it was sounded as though it was serious based on the tone he was using.

"I love you. I would do anything for you, but you already know that, right?"

"I love you too, Penn."

He tilted my face towards his and looked into my eyes. Penn shook his head as though I wasn't quite understanding him.

"No, I love you like I want to be with you forever. I never want us to be apart. Like I'm so deeply, crazily in love with you, it hurts." Penn swallowed hard. "And I have been for a very long time. I just had to say it."

It wasn't like his feelings for me were new, but for some reason, he wanted to declare them as clearly as possible. Maybe it was because of what happened to Carter… he knew our time was limited.

"You don't have to say it back, I know you don't feel quite the same, and tha —"

"I do though. I love you too. If anything happened to you, I'd—"

"Don't say the word," Penn said shaking his head. "If anything happens to me, you have to go on as long as you can. You have to keep fighting."

His words reminded me of the promise I'd had with Dean and Sienna. The one where if anything happened to one of us, the others would keep going. But, Dean hadn't held up his end of the bargain. If anything happened to Penn, I couldn't promise I would either.

"Please," he said but lowered his gaze. I was pretty sure he could tell I wasn't going to make any deals or promises in those regards with him or anyone. I wasn't even capable of making those kinds of promises anymore. A small frown worked across his face as if he'd read my mind. "Get some rest."

Penn let out a heavy sigh, and I turned so I could look into his eyes. I put my hands on the back of his neck and pulled him close. I squeezed my eyes shut as I kissed him so hard my body tingled everywhere. It was as though that was the only way I could let him know exactly how strongly I felt about him.

He wrapped his arms around my waist and pulled me closer. I wasn't even sure we needed the thermal blanket to stay warm when we had each other.

The love he had for me filled the air. It was so strong it was like I could just reach out and touch it. There wasn't anything he had to say or do, I was his... forever.

I wished we could have been back at

our place, together in our warm bed, instead of cramped up in this small, dirt-coated hidey-hole. Penn smiled at me, and I was pretty sure he'd had the exact same thought.

He closed his eyes and took a breath as though he had to calm himself. Penn smiled and tucked me back into his arm. "OK, time for rest. I want to make it back tomorrow."

He wasn't the only one that wanted that. I didn't want to have to spend another night in the woods.

It all felt different though. We weren't bringing Carter back with us. From now on, it would just be Penn and me... our safe place was going to feel so empty, and maybe even a little less safe, without him. I forced myself to stop thinking about Carter, because if I didn't, I wouldn't ever be able to fall asleep. Maybe, wherever he was, he was seeing his sister again. Maybe they were happy, even if I wasn't.

Chapter seventeen.

Relief washed over me when I finally saw our house come into view. Even though I knew I shouldn't, I felt safer just seeing the familiar building. It was ours, but that didn't make it safe.

Once we got close enough, I started to run towards it. All I could think about was getting inside and locking the door behind me. I wanted to shut out the world and exist only in our space.

"Hey! Wait up," Penn shouted.

I turned around wearing a big smile on my face, but he wasn't wearing the same expression. His was something else completely. Worry… concern… apprehension.

I slowed my pace and narrowed my eyes. "What's wrong?"

"Just want to check it out first," Penn said. He didn't say why out loud, but I knew his reason. Penn was worried

154

someone might have come in while we were gone. Maybe he was worried HOME had come back and checked out our place. Or maybe he was worried they were still there.

I followed him as he walked around the outside. His eyes scanned the ground as much, if not more, than they did the house.

"No footprints," he said stopping at the front door. He turned the handle, but it stopped. "Still locked."

"Good."

"Probably."

Penn pulled out his gun and unlocked the door. He stretched out his arm to block me from walking around him and into the house.

Once we were inside, I closed the door and pulled out my gun. I followed Penn as he methodically made his way through our space. Even when he went into the basement and into the tunnels, I tagged along.

It felt as though I had held my breath the whole time, only breathing again once he tucked his gun back into his waistband. "All clear," he said with a forced, tight-lipped smile. "I think I'm going to stay down here for a bit. Want me to walk you up?"

"No, you don't have to do that. It's all clear remember? I'll be fine," I said forcing myself to stop talking.

Penn probably wanted to stay in the basement and dig so he could take his mind off of Carter. Or maybe he wanted to somehow process what had happened so he could come to terms with it and go forward.

"Hey, Ros?" Penn said glancing over his shoulder when I was halfway up the built-in ladder.

"Yeah?" I twisted my head around so I could see him.

"Maybe you should go through our supplies, see what we should store down here in case of an emergency. I mean you don't have to, but if you want something to do."

"Sure. Like what?"

"Water, food items, whatever necessities we might need if we had to spend a long time down here."

I nodded and climbed up the rest of the way. In a matter of seconds, his shovel was roughly pounding into the dirt as he worked on the tunnel.

Penn should have probably taken some time off after everything with Carter, and then the man, but I wasn't about to

156

suggest it to him. At least not yet. If he wanted his space, I'd give him space.

I started going through our supplies like he suggested. I moved things to the side that I thought Penn might want to be hidden in the tunnel.

When there were fewer items on the shelves would Penn think he'd need to go on a run? Maybe going through everything right now was a mistake.

I reached up and found several packages of dried fruit hidden at the top of the shelf. A quivering smile stretched across my face, and it didn't take long for the tears to start flowing.

My knees felt weak. I dropped down to the floor and hugged myself as the tears streamed out of my eyes.

Carter loved dried fruit. There were so many things here that would remind me of him.

When we'd lost the others, we'd always kept moving. It was like we were moving away from the pain of their loss, but inside the home that I'd shared with Carter, it was different. I couldn't move away from the pain.

I couldn't shake the feeling that if I waited long enough, there might be a secret knock at the door. It would be Carter waiting on the other side wearing his handsome smile. He'd look at me with his head tilted to the side and ask what took so long before stomping inside. Then minutes later he'd ask Penn what he could do to help.

No matter how vivid the images, I knew that wasn't going to happen. Like the rest, Carter was really gone.

I quickly wiped the tears away with the back of my hands. This was already hard enough on Penn... I didn't want him to come up and see me crying.

I cleared my throat. "Hey, um, Penn?" I shouted when there was a pause between the digging noises.

"Yeah?" he said with a small cough.

"We're going to have to refill some of these water jugs. Should I go do that, or—"

"How many?"

"Like six. Gallon size," I said, surprised there were that many that hadn't been refilled. Penn had usually been on top of our supplies, but I guess while Carter had been out on the run, Penn's mind had been elsewhere.

It wasn't like we were in any danger of running out. We had tons of water bottles that still had water inside, but for Penn, it was something I knew he'd want to take care of.

"No. Don't go out there alone, Ros," he said, his voice hard and severe.

It wasn't like I had really wanted to, but I wanted to be helpful. I didn't want him to have to worry about something I could handle.

"We'll just do it in the morning, OK?" he asked.

"Sure. I'm going up, want to join me?" I asked, but I already knew what his answer would be.

"Nah, go ahead. I'll be up soon." When the shoveling noises started up again, I went up the stairs.

I walked over to the fireplace to get a fire going. The least I could do for Penn was to make him a warm meal.

I went through the cabinets and found a box of mac and cheese. It wouldn't be quite as good without the butter and milk, but at least it would be hot, and different from the bars we'd been eating.

After it was finished, I walked over to the top of the stairs. He was still working. I considered calling down to him, but instead, I decided to let him be. I set down the bowl of noodles on the table and went to bed.

If he was hungry when he finished, he could reheat them. Maybe the best thing for him wasn't a warm meal, it was just giving him some time.

He'd come up when he was ready. At least I hoped he would.

Chapter eighteen.

In the morning when I woke, Penn was lying next to me. Apparently, I had been so tired I hadn't heard him climb into bed.

I softly walked over to the window and peeked out between the curtains. The snow had started again. Big, white flakes fell from the sky making it hard to see out past our property.

"Sorry," Penn said sitting up, stretching his arms over his head. "Ugh," he moaned as he rubbed his shoulders.

"Too much shoveling," I said turning back to the window.

"Guess so. Sorry, I missed dinner."

I looked at him, wearing a strange tight-lipped smile. "Don't worry about it."

He opened his mouth as if he was going to explain, but I didn't need him to. I wondered if when he snapped his mouth shut, he had realized the same thing.

Penn sat down on the bed and reached forward, picking his pants up off of the floor. I couldn't help but stare at the tattoo on his back.

It was a reminder of how Penn and I had met. After everything we'd been through, I didn't have a single doubt about him, yet anyone else out there with that mark, I'd never be able to trust.

He looked over his shoulder and caught me staring at his marked skin. He quickly pulled on his shirt and walked over to me.

"You know that's not who I am, right?" Penn said staring into my eyes.

"That would be quite a long con." I let out a small laugh, but he didn't seem to think it was funny.

"Ros, I'm serious."

I shook my head almost annoyed he even had to ask. "Of course, I know."

"I wish I didn't have it. How could I have been so stupid?"

Penn walked away from me and looked out of the window. He watched the falling snow. I wondered if he was thinking back to when he'd traveled through the brutal winter and came upon the place I was staying.

That was all another lifetime.

"You are far from stupid," I said standing at his side, linking my arms into his. "The only reason I'm still alive is because of you."

"I wish that were true."

"It is!"

He shook his head side to side. "You don't give yourself nearly enough credit. All you've done. All you've been through. Yet, you keep fighting."

"It's all been luck. My turn is coming."

"Don't say that!" Penn said, his eyes filled with fire and anger. "We can do this."

He slid his hands around my neck and pulled me in for a kiss. It was hard and filled with passion. Every time he kissed me I could feel just how strong his passion for me was, and it was always so... overwhelming. My heart rate increased. My spine tingled. All of the bad stuff around us started to fade away.

I kissed him back, but I feared I couldn't transmit my feelings as well as he could. Even if I felt them just the same.

"Come on," he said taking a step back. "Before I throw you down on that bed."

"And that would be a bad thing?" I asked raising my eyebrow.

He practically growled before he lifted me a foot off of the ground and moved me over to the bed. We both fell backward, his lips instantly finding mine.

I found comfort being with him. His desire was thrilling. It sent a rush through my entire body. There wasn't anywhere else in the whole world I would have rather been.

I wanted to be with Penn for the rest of my life. No matter how long, or short, it would be, I just knew it had to be spent with him.

It was probably an hour later when he stopped stroking my hair. "We should probably go fill those water bottles," he said placing a long kiss on the top of my head. "Ready?"

"Yeah, sure." I sat up with the blanket wrapped around my body as I looked around the floor for my clothing.

Penn was already dressed by the time I finished gathering up my clothes. He stood at the window with his back to me.

"Still snowing," he announced, tapping his finger on the windowpane. "Guess it's going to be another long winter."

164

"It's not as cold as the last one. At least I don't think so, do you?" I pulled on my socks watching him as he studied the falling snow.

"No, definitely not. I don't know how I ever survived those temperatures."

I'd been stuck in the shelter during that first winter after the storms, but I could remember how snow and ice-covered everything was. I hadn't felt the bitter cold like Penn had, but I knew it had been extremely cold.

Penn looked at me and blinked. It was as though he was coming back to the present from being stuck inside his thoughts of the past. He looked me up and down. "Let's go."

I nodded and followed him to the basement. We gathered the jugs, put on our boots and jackets, and went outside.

The snowflakes that landed on my face felt like cold ice shavings, each one prickling my skin. I shivered and swiftly helped Penn put the jugs into the rusted, snow-covered wheelbarrow.

"Take out your gun," Penn said, as he lifted the handles. "Just in case."

I nodded and followed his instruction. We walked to the lake together, Penn leading the way, as I scanned the area around us for anything out of the ordinary. Although, of course, I knew Penn was doing exactly the same thing, only his gun was in his waistband.

The area was quiet. No dog-beast howls, the only thing I could hear was the branches overhead cracking slightly when the breeze caused them to bump into one another.

When we got to the lake, Penn took his gun out and surveyed the area as well. I couldn't help but think of the time I was at the dock, when the man who almost killed me had snuck up on me. If it hadn't been for that man, I wouldn't have ever been saved by HOME and taken to the facility.

"You fill, I'll watch," he said slowly turning his head side to side.

"Maybe we should just go back and melt snow," I said feeling nervous.

"This is quicker. I'm right here." Penn met my eyes. It was as though he knew what was on my mind.

I forced a weak smile and nodded my head quickly.

The dock was mostly visible, but the wooden boards were coated with a thin layer of ice. Sometimes when we came to the dock, there was a buildup of snow around the banks so thick we couldn't see the dock or get to the water, but this time it wasn't much. The water must have been warmer. Hopefully that was a good sign, and maybe winter would come to an end soon.

I carefully walked out onto the boards, trying to maintain my balance. The last thing I wanted was to slip and fall into the water. Even if it was warmer, it wasn't by any stretch of the imagination, warm.

"Careful," Penn said watching me for a second before turning back.

"Trying," I said softly. I was too busy concentrating to worry about the volume of my voice.

I filled the first bottle with the cool liquid and then the second. My fingers were nearly red from getting splashed with the cold lake water. Penn watched me out of the corner of his eye. If I slipped, I knew he'd be jumping in after me.

I grabbed the next two bottles and made my way back to the water. When I heard a strange noise, I stopped moving. I turned to look at Penn who was moving his head, and gun, around trying to figure out where the noise was coming from.

"Come here," he said in a soft but

stern voice.

I turned and shuffled my way across the iced-over boards. Whatever was making the noise was getting louder which, I could only assume, meant it was getting closer.

Right as I was nearing the end of the dock, I slipped and fell face-first, dropping one of the jugs. It bounced twice along the dock before falling into the lake. I quickly reached out for it and almost slid right off the dock.

"Don't worry about it," Penn said walking towards me. He slipped his hands under my arms and lifted me off of the ground with ease.

He pushed the wheelbarrow towards the nearby grouping of trees. The same grouping I'd been dragged through by the man that kidnapped me. I tried to follow, but my feet felt as though they were sticking to the snow.

"Penn," I said feeling as though I was about to get swept away into my thoughts.

"You're with me. You'll be OK." He looked back over his shoulder and locked eyes with me. It took me a second, but then I was back to myself, running alongside him.

Penn pushed the wheelbarrow into a

barren shrub. He crouched down behind it and pulled at my jacket until I was right next to him.

"It's a boat," he said, but I still couldn't see it.

"A boat?"

He nodded and by the look in his eyes I knew he hadn't spotted it yet, he'd only recognized the sounds. After about a minute, I could hear voices although I couldn't make out what they were saying.

"They found the jug. Shit. They are looking at the dock," Penn said, squinting out towards the water.

I wanted to ask what we should do, but I was too afraid to speak. They probably wouldn't be able to hear me at their distance over the boat's motor, but I didn't want to risk it.

They shouted back and forth a bit before motoring away. I watched as Penn's eyes moved along following the boat.

They left.

"Do you think it was HOME?" I asked. I was pretty sure the only people that would have a boat would be HOME.

"Not sure, but I'd put my money on it."

"I don't think that's saying much."

Penn flashed me a half-smile and raised his eyebrow. "Right. I'd put my gun on it then."

"What do you suppose they were doing?"

Penn shook his head. "Working on their expansion project. Come on, let's go back."

"What about the water?"

"Another time. It's not essential."

I shrugged. "It's not like they'll come back this way so soon. At least I don't think they would."

"You're probably right, but if they do, I don't want to be here. I'd rather have us inside with access to our little panic room." Penn picked up the handles and started pushing the wheelbarrow through the snow.

"And the unfinished tunnel."

Penn stared at me for a moment. It seemed as though he was trying to decide if I was making fun of the tunnel, which of course I wasn't.

"I just meant I didn't want to be stuck underground forever. I tried that whole underground thing already, and I wouldn't be excited to do it again."

Penn laughed. "You were living it up then. Our little room is just dirt and supplies."

"I'd lose my mind." I crossed my arms in front of my chest and shivered. It might have been from the cold, or because the idea of being stuck underground again was so unappealing.

"Well, it's not like they'd stay forever. They'd probably check out the place. Then they'd either find our secret location, or they wouldn't," Penn said parking the wheelbarrow in the same spot by the house he always did.

"They'd find our supplies."

"Yeah. Right. And they'd probably take them." Penn unlocked the front door and brought the water bottles inside. Once we were in, he locked the door and checked it twice to make sure it was secure. "Then they'd leave. They wouldn't have any reason to stick around."

"And if they found us?"

"They'd kill us," Penn said looking into my eyes. There wasn't any fear in his eyes, about the idea of HOME finding us. Maybe he thought it was only a matter of time before they did. "Or worse... they'd take us with them."

Chapter nineteen.

While we ate dinner, Penn talked about how worried he was that HOME was expanding. It was unusual for him to be so open with his thoughts. But maybe it was because it was just us. He wanted me to be as prepared and informed as possible.

"I don't know how much longer we have until they find us," he said shaking his head. "And when they do, we need to be ready for them."

"What do you mean by that exactly?"

"I'm not sure yet," he said with a chuckle. "We have to be ready to do what it takes, but beyond that, I don't know what we can do. We have the random traps, and the alarms, but once they're here, we have to either fight or get down into the tunnels as fast as possible and without making any noise."

I shook my head and waved my hand out towards the living room, and then towards the kitchen. "This whole place

172

looks lived in. They'll know."

"Right. But we'll have to hope that they think we're out. That we'd gone somewhere. We have to hope HOME will take what they want and then leave."

I flipped the rice that was on my fork over and watched the sticky pieces fall back down onto my plate like heavy chunks of snow. "The hideout is very well hidden."

"But they're HOME. They taught me everything I know, and I'm the one that came up with the idea. It wouldn't surprise me if they found it." Penn ate several forkfuls in quick succession. "And you shouldn't be either."

"I wouldn't be surprised," I said with a yawn.

"Tired?"

I nodded. "I guess so, but I'm not sure why."

"Still working on getting caught up from our travels," Penn said quickly shoving more rice into his mouth. He was eating like he hadn't eaten in days.

"Hungry?"

Penn smiled. "Yeah, but I'm not sure why." He stopped eating and looked at me. "Sure wish we could lay on the sofa and watch a movie together, or something."

"Yeah, that would be nice, wouldn't it?"

He reached across the table and took my hand into his. "Guess we'll just have to curl up in bed together instead."

I smiled at him knowing exactly what was on his mind. But when I yawned again, he shook his hand and looked down at the small amount of food left on his plate.

"And sleep," he said.

"Sorry," I said quickly covering my mouth. "But I'm not *that* tired."

I wanted to be in Penn's arms again. When we were together, I was able to feel something. It reminded me that I was still alive. Feeling just how much Penn loved me was addicting and comforting… and I wanted more.

I stood up and walked over to his side of the table. I held my hand out to him, and even though he wasn't quite done eating, he didn't hesitate. He grabbed my hand and spun me around until I was pressed up against his chest.

My heart raced when he looked down into my eyes. "The things you do to me," he said as his eyes filled with desire. "Only you."

We stumbled into the bedroom,

174

tripping over our own feet but somehow maintaining balance. As we flopped down on the bed together, I thought about how much I loved Penn too. I wished I could tell him in a way that he'd just know without a single doubt. Everything I felt towards him was just as powerful and deep as what he felt for me.

I loved him. He loved me. I wanted him to know it and feel it just as strongly as I did.

When we were wrapped up in each other's arms, everything felt perfect. Being together in that way was everything I wanted and more.

When we were coming down from the clouds, I rolled onto my back and let out a heavy sigh. "That was so amazing."

"Mmm hmm," Penn said, his chest moving with each deep breath.

I propped myself up on my elbow and ran my fingertips down his bare, solid chest. "I love you."

He looked into my eyes and swallowed hard. "I love you too. Always."

Penn pulled me down against his body and twirled my hair around his fingers. If only it could be like this forever.

I yawned, and I was pretty sure I was

about to fall asleep with a big, happy smile on my face. Hopefully, Penn had one too.

* * *

The next morning, before Penn woke up, I tiptoed out of the room so that I could take a bath. I didn't want him to worry about the additional water we'd have to get. We lived right next to a lake… sooner rather than later we'd be able to replace the water.

Taking a bath was quite unpleasant but absolutely necessary. It consisted of pouring unheated water over myself in the freezing bathroom. I could have warmed the water in the fireplace, but it would have taken too long. Penn would wake soon.

When he lightly tapped a knuckle on the door, my body jerked so sharply I almost knocked half of the bottle of water on the floor. Somehow I managed to snatch it up without spilling a drop.

"You in there?" Penn asked his voice still thick with sleep.

"Yeah, be out in a second," I said twisting the cap back on the top of the still half full water bottle. I grabbed a towel and quickly dried off.

"No, it's fine. Just woke up and you weren't there."

I stepped onto the cold linoleum floor and pulled on a fresh pair of clothes trying to get warm. Even when I was fully dressed, my entire body still shivered uncontrollably. It wasn't my first time bathing in here, I knew it would take a while to warm up again.

When I got into the living room, Penn was putting on his boots. "Are you going somewhere?"

"Just going to check things out," he said holding up a pair of binoculars. "Get your coat on... I'll show you."

"OK," I said happily pulling on my jacket. Hopefully, it would help my body warm up, although going outside wasn't going to help much. "What are you going to do?"

"Carter helped me build a little lookout up in the big tree out front. We must have done that when you were taken," Penn said swallowing. I wasn't sure if it was because he'd mentioned Carter or if he was thinking back to when I had been missing.

He looked out the windows for

several minutes before opening the door. His hand was hovering just over his gun.

"No snow today," Penn said.

"Good."

I followed him out the door and over to the big tree. The brisk air stung my cheeks while the scent of pine filled my nose.

"We nailed these in… they are quite secure," Penn said gesturing towards the slabs of wood that were attached to the tree. It was like a ladder that would take us right up to our tree-house. "You can come up too."

"I can?"

"Sure, there's a floor up there. Watch your step," he said with a little smile.

"I can't believe I'm first hearing about this now."

Penn's smile faded. "Haven't used it in awhile. Probably since you returned."

I nodded, and Penn slipped the binoculars strap around his neck. He started to climb up, pushing away the branches that got in his way.

I followed, climbing up behind him even though the snow from his steps was annoyingly falling down on me. We went higher in the tree than what I thought was safe. The ground below looked so far away.

"Don't look down," Penn said moving over to make room for me on the little wooden platform.

"How did you do this?"

"With a rope. Pulled the pieces up, nailed it all together. It's safe." He stomped his foot on the wood as if that would somehow comfort me.

Our house looked so small from where we were in the tree. I turned and looked out at the lake. The crystal blue waters looked beautiful, and thankfully it was free of boats.

I slowly spun around looking at the ground below and then at the treetops that were now at eye level. Penn watched me as I looked at the scenery.

"What's that," I asked narrowing my eyes at something far off in the distance. It was so far away it was hard to make out what I was looking at.

The snow had stopped falling, but the sky still had a gray, cloudy dreariness that made it hard to tell what I was looking at.

"What?" Penn asked turning his head to follow my gaze.

I pointed out towards the horizon. I wasn't sure how far away it was from us, but it had to be a couple miles.

Penn squinted and then held the binoculars up to his eyes. He didn't move for a few minutes, but then hc let them hang back down around his neck. "Shit."

"What is it?"

"HOME. A tower," Penn sad.

I shook my head in disbelief. How could they have constructed their tower so fast? They were just out here looking for a place. It wasn't possible.

"Are you sure? How?" I asked. My body wanted me to climb down the ladder and hide inside our house. It felt like I was out in the open and if they looked hard enough, they'd see us in the tree.

"I'm pretty sure." Penn looked out again with the binoculars. "It must have been there for a while now."

"How far away do you think it is?"

"Two… maybe three miles at the most."

I shook my head trying to keep myself calm. "Can they see us?"

"I don't know."

Penn gestured at the tree trunk, and I started climbing down. My cold, shaking fingers made it slightly harder to hold on as I descended.

When we were both on the ground, he put his hand on my back and guided me towards the house. He kept looking over his shoulder as though he expected HOME to come rushing out at us.

We stepped inside the house, and Penn checked the lock at least three times before standing in front of the window. He stared out the sliver of space between the two sides of the faded curtain looking in the direction of the tower.

"Can you see it?" I asked almost positive there was no way to see that far at ground level.

"No."

"Good. Right?"

Penn nodded slightly. "I guess, but none of this is good."

"Why did they want to build another so close?" I asked.

Penn shook his head. "Your guess is as good as mine."

"What are we going to do?" I asked my voice slightly higher pitched than normal. "We have to move. Do we have to move?"

Penn ran his hand through his hair. He looked down at his feet and then pinched the curtains tightly, so there was no space between them.

I watched as he walked over to the other one and did the same thing. He locked eyes with me.

He took a deep breath and swallowed hard.

"I know exactly what we are going to do."

Chapter twenty.

I shook my head with my hands firmly placed on my hips. "Absolutely not."

"But—"

"I'd rather take what we can carry and find a new place."

"We can't do that. It's too dangerous. And it's not just HOME we have to worry about, but crazy people… the kind that hangs you from a tree just because they feel like it."

Penn paced back and forth in front of me as my leg bounced rapidly up and down. I was so upset it felt like I was moving the whole floor.

His plan would never work. I trusted Penn, but it was just the two of us, we'd never be able to pull it off, even with all his training.

"You want us to… OK, OK, just tell me again," I said, but I wanted to cover my ears.

"First I'll go... alone and learn what I can," Penn said shaking his head.

"Then, you come back, share what you've learned, and we go back to finish them off." I stood up to stop my legs from shaking. "What if there are fifty of them?"

He closed his eyes as if he was visualizing his plan. "We have to attack. It's our only option. If there are fifty of them, we'll have to adjust our strategy, but we can do it."

I stared at him with my mouth hanging open. It seemed to me that Penn had lost his mind. The two of us could never take down fifty HOME army soldiers. They'd be armed. We'd be drastically outnumbered.

"They'll see you coming. It's a lookout tower exactly for that purpose," I said hoping Penn would see the mistakes in his plan.

"With my training, they shouldn't."

"That sounds reassuring." I rolled my eyes.

Penn dragged his hand down his face. He let out a long breath.

"OK, first I'll go, then based on my findings, we'll adjust the plan accordingly," he said putting his hands on my shoulders.

"I can do this."

"What about me? You're just going to leave me here?"

"You have to stay here. It's not safe for you," Penn said avoiding my eyes. "I don't like it any more than you do, probably less, but you will stay here and guard our house. If anything should happen, get into the tunnel."

My breathing quickened. "I know, but what if something happens to you? What if you don't come back? How will I —"

"You will. But I'll come back," he said with a hard nod. "And then we'll go, and together we'll wipe them out and take down that tower."

I turned away from him and crossed my arms. It wasn't like I was about to hide the fact that I didn't want him to go. Carter left, and he didn't come back… I didn't want the same for Penn.

"The guy who took Carter from us is still out there," I said swallowing down a sour taste in my mouth.

Penn nodded. "I can handle him."

"That's probably what Carter thought too," I said softly.

Penn waved his hand in the air as if

he was erasing away all the thoughts about Carter. He didn't want to talk about it any further. All he wanted to do was talk about his plan and then execute it.

"We aren't going to let them win," Penn said wrapping his hands around my middle. "This is our area. They can have all of the rest of it for all I care, but this," Penn pointed at the ground, "this is ours."

"Please, Penn, let me go with you." It sounded like begging, but I couldn't help it. I was afraid of losing him.

Penn pressed his face against my neck, and I could feel him shake his head. He wouldn't ever allow it.

"If someone steps on our property, just one person, what are you going to do?" Penn asked. It was like he was quizzing me.

"Make sure it's just one. Then shoot."

"Good."

"If you are unsure, what are you going to do?"

I stared at the wall and stiffened my jaw. I couldn't help but feel like Penn was abandoning me, even if I understood his plan and his reasoning. "Go into the tunnel."

"And if a lot of them come?"

"Tunnel."

"Perfect."

I turned around to face him, unable to soften my expression. "And what if they set this whole place on fire? Or what if they find me and kill me?"

"I'll find you."

"You'll find me dead."

He hugged me so hard it hurt. "Don't say that," he said with a sniff. "I think it'll be safer for us if I check things out. I won't be gone long."

"How long should I wait before going and looking for you?"

Penn blinked several times and sucked in a sharp breath. "If I don't come back, assume the worst. Whatever you do, don't leave. Stay here. If something should happen and I get deterred, I will come back here as soon as I possibly can, got it?"

"Yes," I said covering my face with my hands. I was already feeling sadness and desperation as though he was already lost. "Fine. Do it. I'll be fine. But you better come back to me."

"Do not leave here. No matter what," Penn said focusing hard on my eyes.

I couldn't stop the tear that fell out of my eye. It started to slowly drip down my cheek, but Penn quickly wiped it away with his thumb.

"You're the toughest person I know," he said with a stiff jaw.

"I'm the only person you know."

He waved at the air as if pushing my words away. "I will come back to you," he said breathing slowly. "No matter what it takes… I will."

The look in his eyes was so intense it almost burned. I knew he would do whatever he could, but Carter probably had tried too. Sometimes, no matter how badly you wanted something — like getting back to the people you loved — it just didn't work out.

"When are you leaving?" I said burying my face in his chest.

"In the morning."

Penn's body stiffened, but he didn't move away from me. I could tell that his mind was already working.

"I'll refill the water bottles before I go," he said. He was probably making a mental checklist of all the things he wanted to do before leaving. I'm sure he wanted to make sure I had everything I would need while he was away.

Penn spent an hour or so packing his

bag and then checking it over several times. If the tower was roughly three miles away, he could make it there and back in a day if he wanted to.

"Why are you taking that?" I asked scrunching up my nose. "It'll just slow you down."

"I want to make sure I have enough in case something doesn't go according to plan." He turned away from me and started repacking the bag again. "Plus I plan to watch them awhile, to see what I can learn."

"How long are you planning to be gone?"

"A few days. Could be more, could be less."

I pressed my fingertips into my temples. "You could be back tonight," I said knowing exactly how whiny I sounded.

"I don't think that will be enough time. I need to gather intel so when we go on offense we have the upper hand."

"Ugh. Fine. Whatever," I groaned as I walked towards the bedroom. I didn't want things to be this way with him when he'd be leaving soon, but I was so damn frustrated. I didn't want to lose him like I had everyone else.

Penn grabbed my hand stopping me

abruptly. "Hey, come on, don't you trust me?"

"Of course I trust you," I said breathing heavily, "it's everything else I don't trust. You're not invincible."

"And I know that. I wouldn't be doing this if I didn't think it was necessary. HOME is like three miles away from us… it's only a matter of time before they come snooping."

"I just wish I could go with you."

"I know, but I'll be faster and more efficient on my own. You'll keep our stuff safe. You've guarded a house like this on your own before, you can do it again," Penn said without blinking. He had more confidence in me than I had in myself.

I looked at my dirty fingernails and started picking at them one at a time. "I was a much different person then."

"Indeed. Look at all you've survived since. You're much stronger," Penn said with a soft smile. "You can do this."

Penn glanced at the window. It was dark, and I knew he'd want to get adequate rest because while he was out there scouting out the situation, he wouldn't. I didn't even want to ask him where he'd sleep because if I knew I'd only worry more.

"I should get some sleep," he said squeezing my hand.

I smiled and followed him into the bedroom.

Chapter twenty-one.

We stood in the doorway staring into one another's eyes. Neither of us said anything.

We didn't need to talk, I already knew he was going and he knew I didn't want him to. Rehashing it all again would only delay things, not change them.

He slid his slightly cool fingers around the back of my neck and pulled me closer. I looked down at his chest. I couldn't handle the intensity in his eyes any longer.

Penn softly pressed his lips to mine and held them there. I didn't want him to move away, because if he did, I would know it was time.

Our kiss felt different. It didn't feel like an I'll see you soon kiss, it was more like a goodbye kiss. A forever goodbye.

"I really should go with you," I said unable to stop my voice from cracking.

If he heard me, he decided it was best to ignore me. And I couldn't argue because maybe it was.

"If anyone comes around here, do not hesitate to shoot. I reloaded your gun, should you need them there are more bullets in the basement," Penn said with a faraway look in his eyes. He was trying to think of anything else important I might need to know while he was away.

"You think I'll need more? It's quite rare to see people around here," I said with a shrug.

"Indeed. But it could happen. I want you to be prepared. And remember if it's more than one, go hide in the tunnel. It's not worth it, even if you think you can handle them. Don't. Promise?"

I nodded.

"Say the words," Penn demanded.

"I promise."

Penn adjusted the knit hat on his head and looked back into my eyes. "Don't leave. Don't even go outside."

"What if the house is on fire?"

"Not funny."

He took a deep breath and looked at his feet. It was almost as though he was having trouble making them move.

"I will be back as soon as I can," Penn said his voice wavering ever so slightly.

I nodded and bit my cheek so the tears wouldn't fall. They would, but I needed them to stay in until he was gone.

He looked away for a second and sniffed before turning back. Penn tilted my chin up, I didn't have a choice but to look at him.

"I love you, Ros," he said. Not only did I hear the words, but I could also feel them pulling at my heart.

"I love you too, Penn."

There was a slight metallic taste in my mouth as I bit a teeny bit too deeply into my cheek. That's what it took not to let the tears fall.

Penn didn't say anything else. He just turned and started walking away. I wanted to call out to him and beg him not to go, but no matter how loudly my insides screamed, my mouth wouldn't open.

He was going for us. With HOME as close as they were, it was dangerous living here. He wanted to make sure we could sleep at night without an additional worry. HOME could have come around at any point, but knowing they were right there, made it different.

Penn was near the fence when he stopped. Maybe he'd changed his mind. Or maybe he'd just forgotten something.

"Close the door," he said turning his head to the side only enough so I could see his profile.

The tears were welling up too much. I wasn't going to be able to hold them back, so I closed the door... and of course, I locked it.

I started to walk to the couch, but my knees were weak. After two more steps, I lowered myself to the ground and cried. All I could think about was how I'd never see Penn again.

I wasn't afraid to handle things on my own, Penn was right about that, I could do it. What I was afraid of was losing the last person I had on my side. The person I loved with every ounce of my being.

When I didn't have anything left to cry out, I stood up. I took a deep breath and straightened my clothes.

I was going to be hopeful that he'd come back. After all, it was Penn, but the only way I could do it right was to go on as though he wouldn't return. I'd spend each day as if it were just me left in the world.

When my stomach settled, I ripped open a package of toaster pastries and had breakfast. I tried to read a book while I ate but I kept getting distracted by the window. About every five minutes I just had to look outside.

Of course, nothing was out there except for the snow-covered ground and his trail of boot prints leading away from the house.

My body was filled with so much worry and anxiety that I just couldn't relax. I didn't know what the hell I'd do with myself if Penn didn't come back.

I crossed my arms and then uncrossed them. It was like I just didn't know what to do with them.

My eyes shifted towards the door, and I noticed the filled water bottles all lined up.

"Of course," I mumbled as I lifted two of the bottles to bring them downstairs. I couldn't even guess when Penn had filled them. Maybe he woke in the middle of the night to take care of it.

It wasn't even like we were short on water. He probably just wanted to make sure I wouldn't take it upon myself to go out and refill the bottles while he was away.

After I finished bringing down the

bottles, I lingered in the basement examining our supplies. I grabbed a notebook off the nearby shelf so I could jot down things we were running low on. It didn't really seem necessary, but at least it would keep me busy.

When I flipped open the notebook, a loose sheet of paper fell out and floated down to the ground. I picked it up and unfolded it.

Inside was a sketch. It took me a few minutes to realize what I was looking at.

"Whoa," I said tracing my finger over the lines.

It was a highly detailed and ambitious drawing of plans for the tunnel, with Carter's initials in the corner. There were rooms and a whole complex system, almost as though Carter was afraid something would go terribly wrong and we might have to live underground for a significant amount of time.

I wondered if Penn had ever seen the drawing. Maybe it was what they were working on before we lost Carter.

I took the drawing with me and climbed down into the room below. The room I'd have to hide in if HOME ever came snooping. I pressed my hand against the cool dirt wall.

Sure enough, the start of the tunnel lined up with the drawing. It seemed like they were actually working on Carter's plan.

I swallowed down a tear at the same time the air seemed to get cold. A shiver ran up and down my spine.

"Carter," I whispered, but of course nothing happened. Penn was gone for a few hours, and I was already losing my mind.

I was ready to leave the chilly tunnels and head back upstairs when I heard the loud crash. The earth shook, and I braced myself looking up at the top of the tunnel, worried it was about to come crashing down on top of me.

The second the earth stopped moving I climbed up the ladder. I had no idea what was going on, but I didn't want to get buried alive.

Chapter twenty-two.

My teeth were clenched so tightly I could feel the muscles pulling at my temples. I darted up the stairs, looking in every direction possible, but I couldn't make sense of the noise.

That was, until it happened again and I saw the flash of light just before the sound rumbled out. I slowly made my way over to the window just in case I was wrong.

When I peeked out between the curtains I didn't see rain pouring down, I saw snow falling from the purple-tinged sky. A thunderstorm, and snow. Thundersnow.

Maybe Penn would turn back, but something told me he wouldn't. If anything, it would probably delay him.

"Dammit." I grabbed a book off the shelf roughly and flopped down on the sofa. I had to do something to pass the time. Hell, if it hadn't been storming, I might have done some digging following Carter's plans, but with the storm going on, I was afraid the

199

whole thing would collapse on top of me with how harshly the ground was shaking with each boom.

The next day after breakfast, I pulled a chair up to the window so I could occasionally look out between the curtains. If Penn, or anyone else for that matter, was encroaching on my territory, I wanted to know as soon as humanly possible. But the whole time I watched out the window the only thing I saw was the trees dancing gently with the wind.

As the hours ticked by the snow slowed. The worst of the storm had passed sometime during the night… it hadn't done anything except be loud.

Penn was probably making progress on his mission, since the lighter weather wouldn't have stopped him. It probably wasn't even bad enough to have slowed him, which to me was good, because the sooner he accomplished what he had set out to do, the sooner he'd come back to me.

The day passed slowly. I stopped to make my meals, work a little on going through our supplies and cleaned the floors. It was surprising just how dirty the kitchen floor had gotten from dragging all the dirt from the basement through. If I could have

vacuumed the carpet in the living room, I
would have.

When I wasn't busying myself with
some random task that wasn't essential, I
was staring out of the window. I hoped I'd
see Penn walking through the trees back to
the house, but of course, I didn't.

The second the sky turned from day
into night, I went to bed. I was lonely and
bored, not to mention everything else I was
trying not to feel. The sooner I went to bed
and started the next day the closer to seeing
Penn I was. That was, if I saw Penn again.

In the morning when I woke, I jerked
up in bed. My fingers tightly gripped the
bedsheets. Somewhere in my mind, I
thought I was sure I'd heard Penn's voice.

"Penn?" I said looking around the
empty room.

Had he come back or had it only been
a dream? I got out of bed and wrapped my
arms around my chilled body. I made my
way through the house, but I was still alone.

"Ugh," I groaned as I sat down in my
chair by the window. I buried my face in
my hands and aggressively rubbed my eyes.
Maybe if I rubbed hard enough, I'd wake up
from this nightmare.

Even though I was getting adequate

sleep, I felt tired. Being alone in this world was exhausting, but at least I knew if Penn didn't come back, I could do it. I could survive. I could manage things on my own… if I had to, at least until it was my turn to go.

I sighed as I looked out the window. Every day my hope diminished. Anything could have happened to him. Penn, while extremely skilled, wasn't invincible. I tried not to think about how he could be out there hanging in a tree just as Carter had been. Or who knows what else could have happened?

I closed my eyes and sucked in a long, deep breath, trying to erase all the bad thoughts. Of course, I wouldn't be able to make them go away until Penn was back with me. When I opened my eyes, I saw something move between two of the trees.

My heart jumped and pounded against my chest. Penn! A smile started to stretch across my face but quickly faded when whatever was out there didn't keep moving towards the house.
Something was out there, I was sure of it, but I was even more sure it wasn't Penn.

Chapter twenty-three.

I stared at the space between the trees, but I couldn't make out anything. Maybe I had only imagined the movement. My mind was playing tricks on me.

Even though I couldn't remember the last time I'd seen any kind of wildlife, maybe that's all it had been. A squirrel, or a bunny hopping from one tree to the next, looking for food… trying to survive.

I blinked, and when I opened my eyes again, I caught the movement again out of the corner of my eye. I sharply stepped back. It felt as though my heart had actually paused a beat. Whatever it was that was out there, was now closer to the house, lurking near the trees.

I carefully pulled open the curtains and slowly closed them again when I spotted what was in our yard. Standing in the grass was a tall, but thin dog-beast sniffing at the ground.

203

I took deliberate, quiet steps as I made my way over to the next window. My fingers shook as I touched the rough fabric.

As I pulled it open far enough to get a glimpse, my mouth dropped wide open. I put the curtain back in place, attempting not to make any sudden, noticeable movements.

There was another dog-beast wandering around the yard. I was afraid of what I'd find when I looked out of the other windows. My breathing was ragged as I made my way over to the window near the kitchen. I covered my mouth before I opened the curtains.

There were two more dog-beasts walking side by side heading towards the garage behind the house. One of the beasts started to turn its head towards the house, and I quickly closed the curtain.

My eyes were wide as I stared at the curtain as it swayed slightly back and forth until it settled into place. I took a step away from the window, hoping the dog-beast hadn't noticed the movement.

My body was absolutely still, and I tried to remain as calm as I possibly could. Why were the dog-beasts out there? What were they doing here? I tried to remember how many I'd seen… four, five? I couldn't remember exactly, and maybe it didn't matter, there could have been more that I hadn't seen. All that mattered was that they were out there and as far as I was concerned, one was too many.

I took another step back towards the bedroom without taking my eyes off of the window. A dark shadow appeared at the bottom of the pane. I could tell by the shape, it was a dog-beast's head.

Was it trying to look inside? Had it seen me? If it had, I was sure it would have been growling, but I didn't hear anything.

After a few more seconds, the shadow turned to the side and vanished. It left the window area, but I knew it was still out there.

I turned around and tip-toed as quickly as I could to the bedroom window. When I was a foot away from the window, I stopped. I was suddenly too afraid to open the curtain.

I waited.

And waited.

When the shadow popped up, I turned to the side and pressed myself back against the wall, almost as if I was trying to melt away inside of it. I covered my mouth with both hands. I wanted to make sure I didn't make any noise. Hell, I didn't even want it to hear me breathing if it even could through the wall.

The dog-beast only stayed at the window for a few seconds before the shadow moved away. I was still far too afraid to look out the window, even though I wanted to know how bad the situation was.

I tried not to think about what would happen if Penn came back with all the dog-beasts surrounding our house. He'd have to gun them down, which would surely draw too much attention, not to mention I wasn't even sure if he could take them all out.

Maybe we were far enough away from HOME's tower that they wouldn't be able to hear the gunshots. Or the cries from the dying dog-beasts.

I took a deep breath and slid myself closer to the window. I twisted my neck, trying to see out without moving the curtain, but I couldn't. If I wanted to see what was out there, I'd have to just look.

Maybe it didn't matter how many were out there. I already knew it was too many. It wasn't like I could shoot all the dog-beasts. I needed to get rid of them before Penn came back, but I didn't know how.

I sighed and carefully peeked out of the window. There were at least three more dog-beasts out there. Though, they could have been the same dog-beasts from the front of the house, having circled around to the back… it wasn't like I could tell them apart. They all looked the same to me.

"Dammit," I murmured, slowly putting the curtain back into place.

I walked into the living room staying away from the windows. There had to be something I could do to get rid of them. But I couldn't think of a damn thing.

All I could think about was Penn coming back and unknowingly walking right into the pack of hungry dog-beasts. Because that's exactly what they were, hungry. And if they were hungry that probably also meant that they were angry… and desperate.

I ran down the stairs and started rummaging through our supplies. Maybe there was something I'd missed… something I could use to get rid of them.

I grabbed a package of crackers off of the shelf and threw it at the concrete wall. The box dented inward at the corner and fell to the ground with a thud.

There wasn't a damn thing in the basement I could use to get rid of them, and

I knew it. If Penn would have been here, he'd know what to do, or he'd at least figure it out, but he wasn't here. It was just me, and I was clueless.

I made my way back up the stairs, taking each step with careful thought as though the dog-beasts outside might hear one of the steps creak. If they did, they'd of course work together and break down the door to get to me. At least that's what I imagined would happen.

When I stepped into the kitchen, I could see the dog-beast shadow at the window near the dining room table again. I froze in place.

I let out a slow, controlled breath. There was a part of me that had hoped they would have left while I was downstairs looking for a way to kill them.

When the dog-beast moved away, I quietly dashed to the sofa and sat down. I hugged myself as my eyes darted from window to window. They were just as quiet out there as I was trying to be inside. Maybe they were stalking their prey.

I sat there for what felt like several hours, barely moving, until I finally got brave enough to get up. There hadn't been a shadow at any of the windows since I'd sat down. I hoped that meant they had moved on.

"Ooooh," I breathed as I crept towards the window by the door. My fingers were shaking as I reached out for the curtain.

I paused when my fingers brushed against the rough fabric. My stomach started to swirl as if someone turned it to the spin cycle. But I had to know. I had to know if they were still out there.

I shifted the curtain a hair to the side and looked out. The sky was turning dark gray. It would be night soon. Mostly time passed by rather slowly, but with the dog-beasts out there it seemed to be speeding up.

My eyes moved across the yard scanning every inch as thoroughly as I could from behind the curtain. There wasn't a single dog-beast out there that I could see.

I walked over to the window near the dining room table to get another perspective. My palms were sweating, and it felt as though my pulse was in my throat, but I pulled open the curtain anyway.

The dog-beast jumped up and slammed its paws into the glass. I couldn't help but let out a small scream before I was able to clamp my hand down over my mouth.

There was no doubt about it… the dog-beast had seen me.

It started growling and barking as it pounded its thick paws against the window. The whole window rattled so hard I thought it was going to shatter into a million pieces.

I didn't look, but I knew all the other dog-beasts were joining it. There were shadows at both windows by the front door and one at the window near the table.

I looked into the bedroom, and of course, there was one at that window too. Each one making its own distinct noise as if they were taking turns communicating.

"Go away!" I shouted. "Leave me alone!"

I spun in a circle, not sure where in the house I should go. All I saw were their shadows in the windows, and all I could hear were their paws pounding against the glass.

I didn't know how long it would take, but I was pretty sure they'd eventually break their way through. If I didn't think of some way to make them leave, or kill them… I'd be dead.

Chapter twenty-four.

I sat down on the ground with my back against the wall. My palms were pressed against my ears, trying to block out their noises. I didn't want to hear them. Maybe if I couldn't, they'd go away.

The sky was getting darker by the minute. What if Penn came back in the middle of the night with the house surrounded by dog-beasts? It would be so dark… if they were quiet, he wouldn't know they were there.

"He wouldn't," I whispered to myself. It was true, he probably wouldn't travel at night unless he was already very close.

I pushed myself off of the floor and forced myself to the front window. The dog-beasts were still relentlessly barking, howling and pawing at the windows.

There wasn't much of a point in hiding the fact that I was inside, but I only peeked out of a small space between the curtains anyway.

I tried to count them, but they kept moving and jumping around. Maybe six at the front of the house. Either way, it was too many.

I went into the bedroom and pulled an old blanket out of the closet. Instead of lighting the candle on the table like we always had, I plucked it off of the table and brought it downstairs with me.

The basement door squeaked as I pulled it closed behind me. It hadn't been shut in all the time we stayed in this house, at least as far as I could remember.

Closing the thin door hadn't done much to muffle the sounds of the dog-beasts. Each step I took down, they got quieter, but I could still hear them.

If they got inside, the basement door wouldn't stop them. In fact, the shelf covering the opening to the tunnel probably wouldn't stop them either. They'd likely find it much easier than a human would. They'd follow my scent and know exactly where I was.

I spread the blanket out on the ground, lit the candle and sat down on the hard floor. No matter how much I tried not to, I couldn't stop picturing the dog-beasts getting inside.

"Ugh!" I said pushing my fingertips into my temples. I just wanted to think of something I could do to get rid of them, but the only chance I had was to wait it out. All I could do was hope they left before they broke through the door or one of the windows.

If there had been fewer, maybe I would have risked using my gun to take them out. But there were too many, I wouldn't have been able to do it.

While I knew how to use my gun, I hadn't used it a lot. My aim was probably terrible, and I definitely wouldn't have been faster than all the dog-beasts that were out there. They'd take me down in seconds and devour me without giving it a second thought.

I laid down on the blanket and curled my knees towards my chest. Maybe I could get some sleep. And maybe when I woke up, they'd have given up. Maybe they'd be gone.

* * *

When I woke up, I had no idea if it was even morning. Since there were no windows in the basement, I couldn't even guess what time of day it was based on the amount of light in the sky or the placement of the sun. Not that we saw a lot of sun. The only way to know was to go up the stairs and look.

If the dog-beasts were still out there, I couldn't hear them. Maybe they did exactly what I'd hoped, and left, or maybe they were just out there sleeping.

I ascended the stairs as quietly as possible. Each creak the old wood made caused me to pause and listen for their barking.

Nothing.

Quiet.

When I reached the top of the stairs, I slowly turned the handle and opened the door. It was silent other than my breathing.

It was light enough that I could see my way around without the candlelight. Probably the sun had only just started to inch its way over the horizon recently.

The door and all of the windows still seemed to be intact. I was pretty sure they would be, since I hadn't been attacked upon opening the basement door.

If they were still out there, they were absolutely quiet. Maybe when they hadn't been able to break their way inside, they moved on. The only way I could know for sure was to look out one of the windows.

I decided to look out of the bedroom window first. It felt like it was the best choice because if the dog-beasts somehow managed to just then break through the window, I could close the bedroom door and maybe escape downstairs before they tore into my flesh.

"OK," I whispered with a sharp inhale.

I inched towards the window and carefully peeked out between the curtains.

"Dammit," I murmured. I quickly covered my mouth as though I was afraid they could hear me.

They were still out there. Some lying on the ground sleeping or resting, and others walking around looking like they were lost.

Their mouths were hanging open with their tongues sticking out. It looked as though they were having trouble breathing. Another looked as though it was shivering.

One of the dog-beasts started to turn its head towards the window. I stepped back because, as far as I could tell, they'd forgotten all about me. Although, maybe they were just taking a break and would be back to their pounding any minute.

I sat down on the bed, resting my chin on my balled-up fists. My leg was bouncing up and down rapidly as I tried to force myself to stay calm.

What if they wouldn't leave?

They'd given up on trying to get inside, at least so far, maybe eventually they'd just give up entirely and move on? If the dog-beasts were looking for food, they'd have to keep going. The small amount of meat I had on my bones definitely wouldn't satisfy them. Although, if they liked toaster pastries, they could feast for a while on what we had in the basement.

I hugged my knees and started rocking back and forth. As the sun rose and tried to break through the clouds, the world outside continued to get brighter. At least it wasn't storming, then again, maybe that would have chased the dog-beasts away.

My head was down, but I could sense I was being watched. When I looked up, I noticed the dog-ear shaped shadow in the window.

At least one of them remembered I

was inside. Or maybe he had heard the squeak from the bed. Either way, I was back to square one.

In a matter of seconds, the pounding started up again. It was slow at first, and then it grew louder, their cries more desperate.

"It's not like I'm going to let you in," I said, but my voice was quiet. I definitely wasn't intimidating them, not that it would even be possible for me to do that.

I stood up and walked over to the window. I didn't bother to move the curtains, but I balled up my fist and pounded right back.

"Go away!"

The dog-beast shadow jerked away, but then popped right back up. I'd stunned it, but only for a second. When it growled, I could imagine the slobber dripping off of its yellow teeth and its hatred, or maybe just hunger, filled eyes.

"Ugh!" I said pounding my fist against my thigh. I turned to go back downstairs. At least I could kind of pretend they were gone when I was in the basement. Unless I stopped to think about Penn coming back.

He'd probably spot them before they

spotted him. At least I had to hope he would. Penn was good at that kind of stuff. For all I knew, he'd come up with some sort of plan and be able to get right by them.

When I stepped into the kitchen, the pounding stopped. It was suddenly so quiet, I could hear my own heartbeat. My ears started to ring in the silence.

Seconds later, the dog-beasts started whimpering and whining. It sounded as though they were in pain.

I ran back to the bedroom window and didn't hesitate to pull the curtains back. Far in the distance, I could see something moving. A man.

He wasn't walking towards the house. It seemed as though he had no interest whatsoever in coming this way. The man had something between his lips, and I was pretty sure that it was what was causing the dogs to freak out.

I squinted, but I couldn't tell exactly what it was… a dog whistle?

The dog-beasts howled one after the next, and then they started running away from the house, and away from the man. Before long, I couldn't see the man anymore, and I was pretty sure all of the dog-beasts were gone too.

The man didn't know it, but he saved me.

I ran to the front window just to be sure they were all leaving. When I looked out, I pressed my hand to my forehead and smiled.

They were gone. And I was pretty sure they were all gone.

Of course, that didn't mean they wouldn't come back. Even worse, was the fact that Penn was still out there. A pack of desperate, hungry dog-beasts could be heading right for him.

The smile quickly fell off my face. I wished I had a way to warn him.

My stomach was twisted into so many knots I had to skip breakfast. I spent most of the day pacing back and forth in the living room checking the windows. Every time I looked out, I was sure I was going to see the dog-beasts coming back to finish what they started.

I forced myself to sit down. I picked up my book off of the end table, but I couldn't bring myself to read it. It wasn't that I wasn't trying, I just couldn't focus. When I wasn't thinking about the dog-beasts returning, I was thinking about Penn or even other random things that could go wrong at any second.

"Please come home," I whispered. I turned to look at the door, hoping it would swing open, but of course, it didn't.

I'd lost track of how many days Penn had been gone for. It could have been because I hadn't been sleeping well since he'd left, or maybe it was because of the stress of being surrounded by the dog-beasts.

I wanted him to come back. However long it had been, it was too long. He should have been back by now.

There was a sharp whistle through the chimney that caused the flames to dance. The wind had picked up. It was so loud I could hear it howling as it blew past the house.

I slowly walked towards the window, afraid of what I would see when I looked out. But really, there weren't many things that would have been worse than the dog-beasts.

In fact, I could only think of one thing. HOME.

When I opened the curtains, I saw the tree branches whipping back and forth, as thick chunks of snow fell from the sky. It was coming down so fast and so heavy I couldn't even see the fence around our property.

"Oh shit," I said, pressing my hand against the cold glass.

This didn't look good. I slid my feet into my boots and grabbed my coat off of the hook.

Penn was out there. I had to do something. I had to help him.

I checked to make sure I had my key. Then I took a deep breath, opened the door and stepped outside.

Chapter twenty-five.

I stepped out onto the porch. The wind was so cold it felt sharp, like it could actually cut through my skin. Within seconds, I was coated with a thin layer of the chunky snow.

"Penn!" I called out without thinking. What if he was close? What if he was out there wandering around, unable to tell which way he was going? Maybe my voice could help.

I took several more steps away from the house. I wanted to go find him… to do something. Anything.

My entire body shivered from head to toe, both from the cold and from how utterly helpless I felt. There wasn't a damn thing I could do to bring him back home.

If I was going to go, I had to be much smarter. I couldn't just take my boots and coat and wander out into the snowy darkness. I'd need supplies.

"Penn!" I screamed again so loud my

voice cracked. I didn't care if there were any risks.

I stared at the falling snow, hoping that he'd magically appear, my eyes squinting and blinking frantically with each cold snowflake that landed on my face.

"Dammit, where are you?" I said in a much quieter voice.

If he was still out there, I couldn't sense it. I had to believe he was, but at what point did I officially give up on waiting for him? When would I stop looking for him to come back to work on the tunnels, or whatever it was, and start doing those things myself?

Would I even want to go on if it was just me left? I'd made it this far, but what would be the point of going on alone? I didn't have anything to prove, and even if I did, there was no one left to prove it to other than myself.

The wind blew so hard against my body, I had to step to the side to stop myself from tipping over. Each snowflake pricked at my cheeks like a little needle.

"Penn!" I cried out as loudly as I could, but it seemed as though the wind pulled my voice away through the trees.

Shouting probably hadn't been smart,

but then again, I doubted anyone was wandering around in this blizzard. Anyone left would be hiding out somewhere waiting for the storm to pass. They'd be keeping themselves warm, not looking for survivors to hang in trees. Or at least I hoped.

The wind blew again, reminding me of the cold and the snow falling around me. "Please Penn, come back."

I went back inside the house and locked the door. It was surprising how much snow had accumulated on my head and jacket in such a short amount of time.

I stomped my feet and shook the snow off before walking over to the fireplace to add another log to the weakening fire. It crackled and popped as the scent of burning wood filled the air.

I wondered if the dog-beast master had seen the smoke coming out of the chimney when he walked by. If he had, apparently he hadn't cared, at least not enough to come poking around. Maybe he'd put it on his to-do list and would be back, or maybe he'd already been here.

If the fire hadn't been absolutely essential, I wouldn't have started it, but the winter was cold. Without it, I would have been a popsicle.

It was surprising to me that both Penn and Carter had been able to work in the tunnels. I would have thought it would be even colder down there, but perhaps all the shoveling kept them warm because neither of them ever complained about being cold after working.

The wind howled again. It sounded as though it was sad, wailing over something it had lost. I felt like doing the same.

I curled up on the sofa and covered myself with the blanket that had been draped over the back. It was the one Carter had used every night since we made this place our home.

My stomach was twisted in knots, not only from the sadness, but from worrying about Penn. I wanted to go looking for him, but I told him I'd stay here. I roughly knew where the towers were, maybe if I went out there I could find him and bring him back.

Of course, it wasn't like I was stupid. After everything, I knew better. I couldn't go out in this storm. It would be night before I knew it and I'd be out in the cold and dark... it would be suicide to go out there. But all the waiting was killing me anyway.

I kept drifting in and out of sleep. It

was like my body was exhausted from the emotional rollercoaster of the day. My entire being craved rest, but every time the house creaked or the wind whistled, I woke up.

I think I was more than half-asleep when I heard a loud pounding noise near the front door. The gasp that startled me fully awake stuck in my throat.

My heart was racing. It was nearly pitch black in the house. I'd forgotten to light the candle, and the only light was the pale moonlight coming in from outside.

Right when I managed to convince myself that I'd only dreamt the noise, I heard it again. I pulled my gun out from my waistband, keeping it aimed at the floor. I still wasn't entirely sure if what was happening was real or if I was still in a dream.

When someone, or something, slammed into the front door so hard it shook, I knew whatever was happening was real. I swallowed hard. The dog-beasts had come back, or maybe it was their master.

"Stay calm," I murmured trying to keep myself under control. I wasn't sure if I should stay and ready myself, or run downstairs. Once they got inside, all I'd have to do was pull the trigger. "I can do this."

The doorknob rattled, and then there was a knock. I shook my head at the door. The next knock was harder, more aggressive.

"Go away!" I shouted, which was probably a mistake. If I hadn't been half-asleep, I would have probably known better. I hadn't been thinking clearly.

But they didn't go away. Instead, they knocked again… a knock that was slow, but different. It was familiar. A knock I'd heard before.

Chapter twenty-six.

I rolled off of the couch never taking my eyes off of the door. If this was a dream, it was far too realistic. I had to be awake.

I took a step towards the door, my leg felt heavy, and I stepped awkwardly. My leg prickled and poked as the feeling started to work its way back from the knee down.

With each quick step, I grimaced as the knocking grew fainter. Could it really be?

I looked out the window and recognized the clothing and the backpack of the person at the door. My fingers fumbled as I quickly turned the lock and pulled open the door.

Penn practically blew inside as the wind picked up and pushed the door back against the wall so hard I wondered if it broke. He took several weak steps inside before he turned around to close the door behind him.

"So cold," he said pushing the door against the wind. I stepped up next to him to help.

After the door was closed and locked, I turned to Penn. I put my hands on his cheeks and forced him to look at me.

"Crap. You're frozen."

He nodded, and I couldn't help but think back to the time Penn and I first met. He was outside the door, thin and frozen, probably close to death. I was reliving it all over again.

I stood on my tip-toes and pulled his lips to mine. It was like kissing an ice cube.

"Let's get you out of these wet clothes," I said unzipping his jacket.

Penn stared at me as though he couldn't remember what to do to get his limbs to work. "I thought I heard you calling out to me."

"Maybe you did."

Although, that seemed unlikely considering that was hours ago that I foolishly stepped outside. He didn't need to know about that.

"Your fingers," I said pulling the wet gloves off his hands. They were so red. "Can you feel them? Can you move them?"

I tried to keep the panic out of my

voice. Penn held up his hand and looked at it as though it was the first time he'd seen it. He stiffly moved his fingers.

"Come on," I said dragging him closer to the fire, "time to warm up."

He sat there with his teeth chattering. At least he looked better than he had the first time we'd been through all this. This time he just looked cold, instead of both cold and starving to death.

"You need warm clothes," I said keeping my eyes on him as I walked out of the room. I was afraid if I looked away I'd wake up, and he wouldn't be there.

I nervously chewed at the inside of my cheek as I grabbed clothes from his drawer. Each item had a stiff feel from being washed in the bathtub and then hung to air dry. Not that it mattered… all that mattered was that it was dry.

"Here," I said sitting down next to him on the floor.

Penn turned to look at me. His eyes were glassy, but his mouth was no longer vibrating.

"Am I really here?" he said with a half-smile.

"I sure as hell hope so." I smiled back and held out the dry clothes. "Put these on. It'll help."

He ripped off his damp shirt and put on the dry one.

"Pants too," I said.

Penn raised an eyebrow, but I just shook my head. At least his sense of humor hadn't frozen.

He took a deep breath and stood so he could easily change. I didn't look away.

Penn's thighs were just as red as his fingers had been. "Dammit."

"I'm fine," Penn said not bothering to put on the dry pants. I held out a blanket which he tightly wrapped around himself.

"I should get you another blanket," I said, but Penn grabbed my hand to stop me.

"Stay."

He pulled me into the blanket and wrapped it around both of us. Penn held me close, and I pressed my cheek against his chest. It seemed as though I could still feel his frozen body through the thin fabric of the T-shirt.

"How are you?" he said pulling back slightly so he could look at me.

"Perfectly fine. Other than I've been worried sick. Why were you traveling during a blizzard? You know better than that."

231

He shook his head as though he knew he'd made a mistake. "I walked past the last stop, thinking I could make it back. By the time the snow started it was too late. It came on so quickly."

"How lucky are you that you made it back?" I said swallowing down all the what-ifs.

"Quite." Penn kissed my forehead, my cheek and then my lips. It felt as though he was trying to distract me, but I wasn't sure I cared… I was just beyond happy and relieved to have him back. "Anything happen while I was gone?"

I took a step back and crossed my arms. He wasn't going to like it, and I knew he'd stress about it, but I couldn't keep it a secret.

"Something happened," he said knowingly.

"Yes, but everything is fine."

It was his turn to cross his arms, only he did so much slower.

"Dog-beasts flooded the yard. There were so many."

"How many?"

I widened my eyes and quickly shook my head back and forth. It didn't seem to me as though the amount should matter.

232

Any dog-beasts were too many as far as I was concerned.

"Fifteen maybe. I don't know, that's just a guess. It was hard to get an accurate count," I said scratching the side of my head.

"What did they do?"

"They tried to get in, but couldn't."

He nodded. "What did you do?"

I lowered my gaze, feeling kind of embarrassed. "I hid in the basement."

"Good. Where are they now?"

"Gone."

"Yeah, since I wasn't mauled I figured as much," he said with a smirk. "But what made them leave?"

"There was a man."

"Dammit!" he said looking as though he wanted to freak out, but was incapable of it because his bones were still frozen solid.

I put my hand on his arm. "It's fine. He didn't seem to notice or care about the house."

"I don't really understand."

"OK. It seemed as though he was blowing a dog whistle or something, he was too far away to know for sure, but all of a sudden, the dogs started howling and crying. Then they ran off. It looked as though he had them trained, or was trying to. It was weird."

Penn looked down at the floor as though he was in deep thought. After a minute or so he shook his head.

"He could come back. We'll have to be ready," Penn said rubbing his hands together.

I didn't know what he would do if the man came back and I didn't want to think about it. Penn needed to worry about warming himself before he planned how he was going to take out all the dog-beasts and their master.

He paced back and forth in front of the fireplace limping from one leg to the other. After several minutes, he sat down on the sofa.

"So… what did you find out?" I said swallowing hard.

He pushed back his shoulders and looked up at me. "There is a tower, looks pretty poorly constructed, as though it was built fast by people who didn't know exactly what they were doing. There are two buildings at ground level, one they live in and another for supplies. I counted eight men, they took turns working on the tower."

"They didn't see you, I take it?" I

asked as I crossed my arms.

"No, they definitely didn't see me or I wouldn't be back here."

I was already sure I knew the answer, but I wanted confirmation. "It's HOME?"

"Definitely HOME."

"Where are they getting the wood?" I said narrowing my eyes.

Penn shook his head. "I think trees, or from other houses around. I'm really not sure, there was a big pile, but no idea how it got there."

"OK, so, what do we do?"

"We're going to take them, and the tower, out once this blizzard passes," Penn said his face devoid of any emotion whatsoever.

I shook my head not understanding exactly how we were going to take out eight HOME army men and a tower. "What if they send reinforcements? Or rebuild the tower?"

"We'll just keep taking them down again and again and again." Penn drew in a deep breath and stared at me. "Their tower isn't finished. The second it's complete they'll see our house. They'll see the smoke coming out the chimney. I don't have a single doubt they will investigate and do what needs to be done."

"But we have the tunnels."

"We do, but I'd rather it didn't come to that. I don't want them to take our supplies. I don't want to have to start over."

Penn rubbed his hands together like he was conjuring up a devious plan. He knew exactly what we were going to do. If I looked deep enough into his eyes, maybe I'd see the plan playing out like a movie.

"I'll have to show you some moves with a knife. I should be able to handle most of it myself, but just in case something should go wrong you'll need to be able to protect yourself and finish the job," Penn said with a yawn.

"Nothing will happen to you," I said biting my lip. I didn't fully believe it, even Penn wasn't invincible, but I had to say it.

He nodded. "But just in case."

Penn laid down on the sofa, curling up tightly under the blanket. His cheeks were still red, and I was sure he was still cold. I went to the closet and got him another blanket.

After I spread it out over him, I sat down on the floor and rested my head down on the cushion. I could hear his breathing start to slow and I wondered if he'd slept at all since he'd been gone.

The wind whistled through the chimney, and I shivered as though I could feel the cold from outside. There were more blankets, but I didn't want to leave his side.

"We can do this," he said, his voice close to a whisper.

"Sure," I said forcing a tight-lipped smile. "Two versus eight, plus a big wooden tower. No problem."

"We'll arrive at night, they won't even see us coming," Penn said, his words drifting further and further apart as sleep started to take over.

My eyes wouldn't close. Even though I was tired, my body was in overdrive. I still couldn't believe he was back.

Could we really take out HOME? I wasn't sure we had a choice if we wanted to stay here. Maybe it was like this everywhere. Maybe their towers were popping up all over the place and no matter where we went, we'd have to fight.

I didn't want to leave. This was our house. I liked it here. We had to protect it no matter what.

Hopefully, Penn's plan, whatever it was exactly, would work.

Chapter twenty-seven.

The day after Penn came back, he spent more than half of it catching up on sleep. He spent the rest of the time packing one of the backpacks.

The snow had stopped hours ago, and the wind had slowed, but I still wasn't sure we were ready. Everything was moving too quickly. I needed more time to think.

"It's too soon," I said shaking my head. "Your fingers are still pink."

"Ros, I'm fine. I wouldn't do it if I wasn't." Penn sucked in a breath and stood up straight. "I think this should be good. I'll have to carry the gas can too."

"Gas can?"

Penn nodded. "It's in the garage."

"Why do we need a gas can?"

"For the tower," he said looking at me as though he wasn't sure I understood the plan. "It'll make everything easier… quicker."

I crossed my arms and glared at him.

"Of course."

"Here," he said, shoving a hard protein bar against my stomach. "Looks like you could use the energy."

"Me?" I mumbled, and he smirked and turned away.

I took it from him and gnawed at the old stale bar while Penn checked the pack again before zipping it closed. We were only taking one backpack and the gas can. Anything more would slow us down. Penn wanted it to be a quick job — get rid of them, take down the tower, and get the hell out of there.

Penn stood there staring at the pack with his hands on his hips. If I had to guess he was running through all the plays in his playbook to make sure he had picked the right one.

"Are we leaving?" I asked moving my jaw up and down, trying to get the sticky bits of the bar out from between my teeth.

"Not yet."

"Why not?"

He shook his head and walked over to the window. "It's too early. We need to arrive at night."

"You want to travel at night?" I asked narrowing my eyes at him.

239

"I want to arrive there when it's dark."

I shook my head and sat down on the sofa. "You tell me when it's time to go, and I'll follow you."

He sat down next to me rubbing his palms up and down his thighs. It was like he was trying to warm them up. When he caught me watching him, he stopped.

"Are you sure you're OK?" I asked raising an eyebrow.

"Yes," he said. He looked away and shrugged a shoulder. "It feels a little cold and numb, but I can still feel them. I'm fine."

"Frostbite?"

He shook his head. "No… maybe it was close, but no. I'm fine. Really."

"Oh, OK. So, you don't have it yet, but maybe by the time we get back." I crossed my arms and rolled my eyes, which I don't think he noticed.

"Ros, seriously. We have to do this. Even if my legs are a little cold."

"I agree, but it could probably wait another day or two."

"Maybe," Penn said scratching his head. "But maybe not. I don't want to take that risk when it comes to you, or our home."

He turned towards me and took my hand into his. When I wouldn't look at him, he put his thumb on my chin and turned me. I didn't have a choice but to face him.

"I will be OK. I promise."

"You can't promise that," I said feeling both sadness and anger rising within me. I pushed the names that started to rise up out of my mind... the names of those who weren't OK.

He opened his mouth to say something, but snapped it shut. Either he knew I was right, or he just didn't want those names to surface.

"I'm just worried about you. I don't want anything to happen to you, not even frostbite. It was a rough few days without you, I can't even imagine the rest of my life. And I don't want to." I swallowed down the lump that had formed in my throat.

"Do you think it was easy out there for me without you?" Penn asked looking like he was offended. "You were all I thought about. I don't want to think about the what-ifs either, but as long as HOME is this close to us, I can't help but think of some of them."

I looked down at my pale skin against

his still pink fingers. At least they didn't feel as cold as ice cubes any longer.

"If you say you're fine, then I believe you," I said unable to stop the sigh that followed. Penn chose to ignore it.

"Good. Because I am." He blinked several times before catching my eye again. "Are you afraid to go? Because I could try to—"

"No!" I said too loudly. "I am most definitely not scared."

Which was close to the truth. I was a little scared, who wouldn't be? But mostly, I was worried.

"I'm ready when you are," I said.

Penn got up and looked out the window. I could tell he was scanning the yard. "Good," he said and walked over to the sofa. He lowered himself down slightly and kissed the top of my head. "Because it's time."

Penn stuck out his hand, and I took it. He looked me over to make sure I passed his inspection.

"You have your gun?" Penn asked, his head slightly tilted to the side.

"Yes, sir."

"How about the knife?"

"Yes." I patted my hip where he'd

helped attach it to my pants.

He looked down and nodded. "You remember what I showed you?"

When he'd given me the knife, he also took some time to show me how to use it. He showed me on a garbage bag stuffed with trash and a pillow, but I was pretty sure actually having to use it would be quite different.

"Yeah, I think so," I said looking at the shredded-up trash bag in the corner of the room.

"We can practice more if you want," he said but tapped his foot. He was ready to get moving.

I shook my head. "Don't need to."

Penn clapped his hands together, and I jumped. He stared at me for a few seconds. I was sure he could tell just how nervous I was.

"Ready?" he asked with slightly narrowed eyes.

I forced a smile and pushed my shoulders back. "Ready."

Chapter twenty-eight.

I kept looking back at our house as we walked away. Maybe it would be the last time I'd see it.

Our house was the only place that I had felt somewhat safe since having left the shelter forever ago. The unfinished underground tunnels helped to make it feel even safer. If something went wrong, we'd have somewhere to hide.

But here we were, walking away from that safety. Walking right into another one of HOME's lairs. Once we completed our mission, we'd probably be slightly safer for awhile, but I couldn't help but think we were crazy for shaking the bees' nest.

"How are you doing?" I asked glancing at Penn's legs. We'd probably only been walking for an hour or so.

The air was still quite chilly, and the snowflakes were just sporadic flurries that didn't affect our visibility in the least.

Trudging through the snow was difficult, but I didn't think it was slowing us down all that much.

"Perfectly fine," he said pausing between each word. It seemed as though he was annoyed with my question.

"Good. Don't want you to get too cold. You know?"

He nodded.

I had to trust he knew what he was doing. He was from Alaska and had suffered through the first freeze, which had been much worse than what we were experiencing now, but I couldn't help feeling worried. Penn was all I had left.

"I think we're probably about halfway there, if I remember correctly," Penn said keeping his voice low.

"What? Really? Then what took you so long to get back? I was worried sick!" I tried to keep the anger out of my voice, but I was pretty sure I'd failed.

"I observed for a while. Which is how I know they all go to sleep at night. No one keeps watch." Penn shrugged. "Well, at least that's what they did when I was there."

Penn stopped abruptly and turned to the side. I tilted my head, but I didn't speak.

I could tell he was listening to something. Then, I heard it too.

There was an odd rustling noise, but it didn't sound as though it was close. I scanned the area between the trees, but I couldn't see anything except for the brown tree trunks and the white snow covering everything.

I turned to Penn when the noise stopped. He glanced at me and gestured forward.

"What was that?" I asked softly.

He shook his head back and forth slowly. "Not sure."

"HOME?"

Penn took in a slow, heavy breath. "Not sure."

I stopped and turned my head so I could look up at the sky between the branches. It would be dark soon. Everything seemed to be going according to Penn's plan.

I heard his footsteps crunching in the snow, sounding as though they were getting further away. I let out a sharp breath and quickened my pace to catch up.

"You coming?" Penn said glancing back over his shoulder for a second.

"Yeah," I said, but when I took

246

another step, I felt something tug at my middle. Whatever it was quickly tightened before it pulled me backward and then up.

In a matter of seconds, my feet were off the ground, and I was being pulled higher and higher. When I saw the thick rope around my midsection, I tried to flail my arms to break free, but the movement only made the rope tighten more.

"Penn!" I shouted.

The instant I heard the dog-beast's growl, I snapped my mouth shut. Shit.

My eyes darted side to side looking for Penn to step out from behind the trees, or at the very least to give me a signal that he was still with me.

"Stop struggling," a male voice said.

"No!" I screamed back, but he tightened the rope so hard I thought my insides were going to squeeze right out of my body.

The man stepped around my side, and I could see him holding a long pole-like leash which had a dog-beast attached to the far end. He could make the dog-beast go wherever he wanted, and the pole was firm enough that it kept him far enough away. It was his weapon.

I blinked when I saw a blur move past

my vision. At first I thought I was about to get hit with something, but I wasn't. Instead there was suddenly a rope looped around my neck.

"Please," I said breathing heavily.

The man took two steps to the side, and I saw the long metal piece hanging around his neck. A dog whistle. I was pretty sure it was the man who'd been near the house. And considering I was hanging from a tree with a rope around my neck, I was also pretty sure it was the same guy that had killed Carter. If Penn didn't turn back soon, I'd be next.

"Now hold still," the man said shifting the ropes around from one hand to the other. "Gotta do this just right, or you'll fall and choke."

"Isn't that what you want?"

"Got anything on you I should be knowing about?" he asked squinting with one eye.

I shook my head, but I was pretty sure he didn't believe me.

"Tsk, tsk," he said clicking his tongue.

I tried to remember what the man who'd been responsible for Carter had looked like, but my mind was a blur. It just had to be him, and the same thing that happened to Carter was about to happen to me.

"I was just wondering," I said talking a little louder than I probably should have, but I was kind of hoping Penn might hear me and come back to rescue me. Eventually, he'd realize I was gone and come looking… I just had to hope it was sooner rather than later.

The man looked as though he swallowed something sour. "What?"

"Did I do something wrong? Like is this your land? Why are you going to have that thing bite me and then leave me here to die?" I asked. My fingers were starting to go numb.

He stared at me for a moment as though he wasn't sure he understood the question. "You're all just bad. Everyone left. You all just want me dead, but I'll get you first."

"I don't want you dead," I said opening my eyes wider. Although it wasn't exactly true, and now that he had me up in a tree, I kind of wanted him very dead. Not just for me, but for Carter too.

"Doesn't matter kid, not going to fall for your lies. Not this time," he said pointing to a long scar on his cheek. "All my friends are gone. You killed them. It's not going to happen to me is all I know. Unlike them, I was prepared," he said wagging his finger at me as if I was the mastermind behind everything that had ever gone wrong in his life since the day he was born.

"Prepared? How so?"

He flapped his hand at me as though I was wasting his time. All I wanted to do was keep him talking. Penn had to have realized I was gone by now. He'd come back.

"I lived in an underground shelter when everything first happened. The man who built it was a genius. Had everything in there. Running water, fully stocked kitchen… everything," I said trying to make it sound like I was bragging, but it didn't seem to be working the way I'd hoped.

He walked around messing with the ropes, ignoring every single word I'd said, at least he made it seem that way. Though, the man still hadn't told me to shut up.

"Yeah, it was awesome. We were so safe there for the longest time. Bet you don't have anything like that," I said raising an eyebrow.

"Pssssh, weapons, bug-out bag, underground shelter, supplies to last me years to come," he said practically sneering.

I nodded appreciatively, but all I really wanted to do was ask where his place was. It had to be somewhat nearby.

"Not bad. Wish I could see it, bet it doesn't even come close to the accommodations I had. I was practically living in a five-star underground hotel," I said swallowing hard as the rope around my neck tightened. It wasn't working. I was going to be dead soon... well, first I'd be bitten, and then dead.

"Kid, please."

"What? You'd be so—"

"No, I wouldn't."

I cocked my head to the side as much as the rope would allow. "What makes you so sure?"

"If it was that great, you'd still be there," the man said slightly shifting his eyes in my direction. I was pretty sure it was the first time he'd really looked at me, and the first time I looked at him.

He was older, but he wasn't as scary looking as I had originally thought. His hair was gray, and his beard was long, but he looked as though maybe once upon a time,

251

he'd been someone's dad. Someone normal.

"Why do you want to kill me?" I asked. He stared at me, and the dog-beast growled hungrily.

"I'm sorry," he said, looking away from me. "Too risky not to. It's my only option."

I shook my head side to side. "But why the bite? Why not just hang me?"

He looked down at the ground. "This way I can blame the dog."

I let out a small huff. He sounded like Penn. The man's reasons weren't any different, only this time I was on the wrong end of it.

"I understand," I said closing my eyes. I thought the tears would flow, but they didn't.

When I opened my eyes again, the man was staring at me with a strange look on his face. Apparently, he hadn't expected me to be understanding. He also didn't expect Penn to be sneaking up on him.

I wasn't exactly sure what Penn was planning because if he killed the man, he'd let go of the leash and the dog-beast would surely attack me. I'd rather hang to death than get bitten.

Penn expertly stalked the man. He

was as quiet as a mouse and as nimble as a cat. The man had no idea he was there. He was one step behind the man when he made his move.

Penn moved so fast if I would have blinked I would have missed the whole thing. He glided the blade swiftly across the man's neck and rolled his body so he could grab the leash just as the man let go.
Only there was a problem. The pole-like-leash slipped right through his fingers. Penn missed.

Chapter twenty-nine.

The dog-beast took off at full speed towards me. I struggled against the ropes which caused them to tighten. There wasn't much slack left in the rope.

"Penn!" I said. It felt like time had started to slow down, and unfortunately that included Penn.

He was running after the dog-beast, but I knew, and I was pretty sure he knew it too… he wasn't going to catch up in time.

I tried to swing my body side to side even though it was choking me. Maybe if I was a moving target it would make it harder for the dog-beast to leap up and bite me.

My plan was backfiring, because the world around me started to go fuzzy. I wasn't getting enough oxygen.

I saw the blur of the dog-beast as it was about to leap into the air. My eyes shifted towards Penn because he was the last thing I wanted to see before I was poisoned or killed, or whatever was going to happen to me.

His gun was aimed at the dog-beast, and even though I knew he didn't want to shoot, he pulled the trigger. With perfect accuracy, he hit the dog-beast with a lethal shot.

If HOME heard the gunshot, they might come to investigate. But when it came to choosing between my life and HOME potentially finding us, well, I guess he picked me.

With that last thought, everything started to fade to black. I moved my lips to call out to him, but there was no volume to my voice. At least not as far as I could tell.

"Ros!" Penn called from somewhere far, far away.

Every inch of my being was going numb, tingling... disappearing. Even my thoughts started to disintegrate from my mind.

When I hit the cold, snow covered ground everything came rushing back like someone had turned on the lights. The electricity was surging through my body bringing me back to life. The bright light stung my eyes when they popped open. I desperately gasped for air as though I was drowning.

"Ros! Ros!" Penn said moving his head this way and that. My eyes were rolling around, and I knew he was trying to get me to focus on his face.

"Penn," I said, my voice scratchy. He put his hands on my cheeks, but my eyes kept moving. I blinked rapidly until the world around me started to make some kind of sense again. "Cold."

Penn raised me up to a seated position which helped some, but my body still had a strange chill to it, and not just because my legs were still in the cold, wet snow. I shivered when he wrapped his arms around my shoulders.

"Dammit, Ros, you had me scared there for a second," Penn said swallowing so hard I could see the lump move down his throat.

"Only for a second? Felt much longer to me," I said looking at him. I was trying to smile, but I wasn't sure my face was cooperating. I was almost certain the look I was wearing was something quite awkward. "Help me up."

"You sure?"

"Yes," I said shivering again.

Penn put his arms under mine and

lifted me with ease. He held on tightly, not trusting that I would be able to hold myself up.

At first my knees threatened to give out, but it didn't take long to get my strength and balance back. I put my hand on Penn's shoulder to keep myself steady. He watched as I took a careful step away from him.

"OK. OK. I'm… I'm good," I said with a surprised grin. A grin that quickly faded when I saw all the red colored snow all around us. "We should go."

Penn nodded and put his arm around me. He grabbed the backpack and swung it over his shoulder while carrying the gas can in his free hand.

He stopped and made sure I wasn't going to tip over before he took several steps towards the man lying on the ground. His fingers gripped the dog whistle that was still around his neck, and he yanked it off.

Penn tucked the whistle into his front pocket before putting his arm around me again. When our eyes locked, we both nodded.

The sun was providing a little light, but soon it would be gone. Penn hadn't adjusted his travel calculations to include being attacked by the dog-beast master.

"How will we see where we are going?" I asked nodding towards the sun. "I'm slowing us down. We need to walk faster."

"We'll make it," Penn said, but he didn't sound all that convincing.

It wasn't like we could just click on the flashlight, which I was sure Penn had tucked away in the backpack. We would have to navigate through the darkness with nothing to light the way except for the light of the moon.

"I can walk on my own," I said holding my palm up. My body had returned to normal. There weren't any signs, except for maybe around my neck, that I had almost been hanged to death.

Every ten steps or so, Penn would shoot a glance at me. I knew it was because he was worried, but instead of telling him again, I ignored it. It wouldn't matter how many times I told him, he wouldn't believe me anyway.

"How much further do you think?" I asked quietly.

"Not much," he said in a voice even softer.

Thankfully the snow had completely stopped, and the wind had died down to a random breeze. Although neither of which helped my legs any. My calves were sore from trekking through the thick, wet snow.

It hadn't felt like we'd walked that much further when Penn held up his index finger towards the sky and then pointed straight ahead. When our eyes met, he brought his finger to his lips.

We were close. Talking was off limits.

I squinted through the trees, but I still didn't see what we were looking for until Penn abruptly grabbed me and pulled me down behind a large tree trunk that looked like it had been lying there rotting for quite some time. My eyes scanned between the trees, and then I spotted it. I saw the tower.

I looked up over the log and saw both of the buildings, one of which had some supplies scattered on the ground next to it. What I didn't see was people.

Penn was shaking his head back and forth. Either he was wondering where they were, or he had anticipated my question about it.

That's when two older men practically fell out of the poorly built building. They were laughing and playfully shoving one another. I knew instantly they were drunk.

Maybe this was going to be far easier than I initially suspected.

"I gotta take a piss, man," one man said weaving back and forth.

"Then piss," the other one said unzipping his pants. He started relieving himself only a couple feet from the entrance to the building. "Hey, Derrick?"

"Yeah?"

The one that wasn't Derrick zipped his pants and stumbled a few steps closer to the building. "I think Pauly is pissed."

"What makes you say that?" Derrick said stepping out from behind a tree.

"Dick's passed out, and the rest of us playing cards while he's trying to sleep? Man, it's going to make it hell for us come morning."

"Shit." Derrick threw his empty beer bottle into the air aiming at the treetops just above Penn and me. "It's hell even when he isn't pissed."

The one whose name I didn't know stood there with his hands on his hips nodding. The beer bottle crashed into one of the branches behind us and dropped slowly to the ground landing with a soft thud.

When a dog-beast howled nearby,

both men straightened their stance as best as they could in their condition. Their heads moved in every direction just as mine wanted to, but for some reason, I was more afraid to take my eyes off of them.

The other men poured out of the building looking around. They had heard it too, and obviously, they weren't fans of the dog-beasts either.

"They close?" The biggest man asked as he cocked his gun.

"Nah, I don't think so," Derrick said with a smirk, but it looked fake. He looked nervous... afraid.

The one whose name I didn't know stepped forward. "Think it was just one, boss."

I was pretty sure the big one was Pauly, not that it would matter if everything went according to plan.

Pauly snorted and spit out a big wad of mucus into the snow several feet away from where they were standing. He punched Derrick in the arm. "Dumb shits. You know it's never just one. Let's look around. Don't want those things slinking around... don't want to lose another, do we?"

The men shook their heads as they all

pulled out their guns. They started walking around, ducking under branches to check the area.

"Stay here," Penn said so softly, his words drifted by on a light breeze.

By the time I turned to look at him, he was gone. At least this time, when he disappeared, I knew he wasn't abandoning me. I wasn't sure what he was up to, but at least I didn't feel deserted. Well… at least not in the same way as I had other times.

I watched the men moving around the camp, peering out between the trees, only taking a few steps out of the clearing. One of the men stepped towards the tree I was positioned behind.

When he turned away, Penn made his move. He was quick, and so silent the HOME guy was down on the ground lifeless before he even had a chance to call for help.

One down.

Penn disappeared again. A man across the clearing suddenly vanished, and I knew it was because of Penn.

That's two.

Penn had said there were eight men here, with two gone that left six. That still left us outnumbered.

I glanced around the camp, and when

I saw number three vanish practically into thin air, I counted the remaining. Four. Four?

"OK, I think we're good. All clear," the one in charge, Pauly, said and the others started to gather around him. Four. One was missing.

Dammit. Damn it all to hell.

Pauly's eyes narrowed as everyone gathered around. "What the... where did... shit."

When Pauly changed his stance to an aggressive one, the others mimicked him. They looked confused, but I was pretty sure this wasn't good. If Penn didn't do something quickly, they would investigate, and they would find me.

Chapter thirty.

If I moved even the smallest amount, the men would notice. It was so quiet I was sure that they could hear a pin drop, even if it was cushioned by the snow.

"Something's wrong," Pauly said pulling his shoulders back. He looked like an animal getting ready to pounce.

"Maybe they just had to take a piss," Derrick said.

Pauly glared at him. It was obvious even at my distance that he was annoyed.

"All of them? Together?" Pauly said with a sneer. Derrick shrugged, looking as though he didn't think it was out of the realm of possibilities. "Don't be stupid... someone is here."

I couldn't stop thinking about the missing man. Maybe Penn had taken out the extra man somewhere behind the trees and I hadn't seen it. Maybe something else had happened to him... like he went back to the base. All I knew was that there was one less man now than when Penn had done his recon mission only days ago. Hopefully, Penn noticed.

"Spread out," Pauly said, directing everyone in different directions with the barrel of his gun. The last spot he pointed to was exactly where I was hiding.

I took as silent of a breath as I could manage as I readied my gun. Either I'd be found and killed, or I'd have to do whatever it took to survive. Again. My choice was easy, although the resolution I wanted wasn't guaranteed.

As Derrick inched closer, my hand started to shake. No matter how necessary, using my gun, even for my own defense, wasn't easy for me. Of course, that didn't mean I wouldn't pull the trigger if I had to.

"Boss," Derrick said as he squinted between the trees. I was almost sure he'd spotted me... or our gear. Maybe even the gas can nearby, and he was about to alert his boss.

"What?" Pauly hissed as he glanced over trying to see what had grabbed Derrick's attention.

After a few seconds, it seemed as though he noticed too because he started walking in the same direction. I couldn't move. If I did, they'd definitely hear me, or maybe even see me. I wasn't even sure I could move if I wanted to.

Both of their heads turned sharply in another direction when something made a loud noise against a tree across the way. They quickly forgot about me, and three of them moved towards the noise while a forth stayed back trying to look in every direction at once.

It didn't take Penn more than a couple of seconds to make his move on the one that was standing alone. Before his lifeless body hit the ground, Penn was already hiding again somewhere in the trees.

I moved several feet in the opposite direction while the men were distracted, but I was too afraid to go far. I'd make too much noise. Would it even matter if our stuff was still there? They'd know someone was here.

"What the fuck!" Pauly said walking back into the clearing and stepping over the man's body. His expression suddenly changed as if a light switch had been flicked somewhere within him. He knew he wasn't dealing with just anyone. "Stay together."

They all turned until their backs were

touching. The men started to slowly turn in a circle as they looked around. It was almost as if they expected Penn to come flying at them through the air like a superhero.

I wondered if all of them grouped together would make things easier for Penn. Either way, I didn't think he'd have much trouble taking out the remaining three.

I tried to locate Penn within the trees before he acted, but I couldn't. The second the first shot rang out I saw him.

Pop. Pop. Pop.

Each bullet hit its target. Each shot, except for one, was a kill-shot. Pauly was still alive and trying to crawl back inside the building. I couldn't help but wonder if Penn had kept him alive intentionally.

When Pauly spotted Penn he tried to move faster, but it seemed to actually have the opposite effect. It looked as though the snow surrounding him had turned into glue.

Penn grabbed him by the back of his jacket and lifted the bigger man halfway off of the ground. He said several things, but I couldn't hear any of it. I was sure he was asking about the tower or other questions about HOME or their plans, but it didn't matter because when Pauly laughed

267

hysterically, Penn finished the job.

If I had to guess, Pauly wasn't talking.

Penn looked around carefully before stepping into the trees. He nodded at me as he picked up the gas can.

"What was that all about?" I asked still keeping my voice soft. Even though it was dark, I noticed the droplet of blood on Penn's coat.

"Just asking the usual questions about HOME."

"I guess he didn't feel much like talking."

Penn shook his head as he put his hand on my back to guide me along with him. "They never do."

Penn stepped away from me and started pouring the gasoline at the base of the tower. He was working fast. I knew he wanted to get moving as soon as possible after setting everything ablaze.

"What's in there?" I asked trying to peek inside the building. "Anything we could use?"

"Probably," he said but splashed the gasoline all over the front of the supply building. "We don't have time, and it would slow us down to carry it all back. When they come back here, we don't want to make things easy for them."

I nodded as the last drops of the gasoline container dripped out on the side of the main building. Penn tossed the plastic gas can back towards the trees before bending down to ignite the buildings.

It took a couple tries to get the match to light, but once it did, he tossed it into the strong-smelling liquid. The flames grew much quicker than I would have thought possible. I could feel the heat warming my cheeks.

"Let's go," Penn said gesturing towards the trees. "Get the bag."

I turned around and walked away assuming he'd grab the gas can and catch up to me. When I picked up the backpack, I turned around, but he wasn't there.

"Penn?" I whispered loudly into the darkness.

He didn't answer. I was standing alone in the dark with a very intense feeling that something was wrong. I dropped the backpack and cautiously walked back towards the clearing.

Close to the blaze, I spotted Penn. He was about to throw his fist through the air towards a much taller man. When his fist connected with the man's jaw, his head spun to the side and jerked to a stop.

At first he looked angry, but then he started laughing. Why hadn't Penn shot the man? Why were they having a fistfight right next to the flaming tower?

I quickly shifted my eyes down and noticed that both of Penn's hands were empty. It didn't take long for me to spot his black gun standing out against the white snow.

Penn tried to move towards it, but the bigger man kicked it out of his reach. "Haven't you done enough killing for one night?" he bellowed as he punched Penn in the stomach. Penn doubled over. "Me on the other hand? I haven't killed anyone... yet."

Penn coughed several times before he was able to straighten himself. Although it wasn't quite straight... it was easy to see Penn was hurt.

I pulled out my gun and took a step back hoping not to be noticed, but the man grabbed Penn's arm and twisted it hard behind his back. He was using Penn's body as a shield.

"I should have known you wouldn't be alone. You ex-HOME too?" the man asked narrowing his eyes at me.

I quickly nodded, but my shaking hand probably gave away the fact that I was lying through my teeth. My eyes connected with Penn's for a split second and I wasn't sure what I saw in his eyes. It appeared to be something close to worry, but was it worry for me, himself, or both of us?

I would have thought Penn would be able to break free from the hold he was in, but he wasn't able to. He was trying to hide the pain he was in, but the grimace on his face gave it away.

Penn didn't take his eyes off of mine. If he was trying to relay any kind of telepathic message to me, I definitely wasn't receiving it.

"Two ex-HOME, huh? We knew there were still some of you out there. It won't be long until all you damn traitors are eradicated." The man laughed a loud, boisterous cackle.

"We have backup on the way," I said, but my voice wavered slightly. If the man staring at me had ever played poker, he'd easily be able to read my bluff. As I saw it, my only moves were to try to trick him or pull the trigger, and I knew my aim wasn't that good. If I was slightly off, I'd kill

Penn.

The man laughed again. "Sure thing, honey."

The raging fire behind them lit the area brightly. It was almost too hot for me, and I was much farther away from it than Penn and the man were.

"Alright then sweetheart, you gonna do your thing or what?" he asked shifting his weight. The only reason he hadn't already killed Penn was because he knew if he did, he wouldn't survive either. He was probably trying to come up with a plan wherein he could take us both out. I'm sure he had the skills to do so. "Time's running out."

I hated it, but he was right.

"Do it. Pull the trigger," Penn said, the nearby flames reflecting in his eyes.

"Yeah, do it," the man said in a mocking high-pitched voice.

Penn nodded at me as though I was supposed to know exactly what to do, but I didn't. I could see he wanted me to do something, but surely it couldn't be that he actually wanted me to shoot him.

It was an impossible shot. Penn had to know I didn't have the skills to pull it off. I wanted to shake my head but I couldn't with the man watching.

"OK, enough playing around," the man said, and there was something in his eyes. I knew he wasn't kidding when he raised up his hands and positioned them on each side of Penn's head. He was seconds away from snapping his neck, and then, probably, mine.

So, I did it. I wasn't even sure I took the time to check my aim. I just pulled the trigger.

Chapter thirty-one.

They both stared at me. Time didn't seem to be moving at all. I couldn't tell which one looked more surprised that I had actually done it.

When the bullet from my gun hit the man in the arm, Penn was able to break free. The second he was several steps away from him, I shot again. And then again.

Penn picked his gun up off of the ground and turned towards the man, but he was already lying face down in the snow. He wasn't moving. I lowered my gun and watched Penn kick the man, with his gun pointed right at the man's head.

"Thanks," Penn said as he pulled me along back into the trees and away from the raging fire. "Now let's get the hell out of here."

Penn picked up the gas can and backpack and grabbed my hand. His eyes were focused on the engulfed buildings behind us. I looked over my shoulder and saw a piece of the tower break off. It started to fall towards the ground, but before it landed, Penn pulled me away.

We walked fast. I wasn't sure where I was getting the energy from, but I kept up with his quick pace.

Despite everything that had just happened, there was a big smile on my face. To me, it felt like we had finally, albeit temporarily, defeated HOME. This time we hadn't run away. We went headfirst and took them down.

In the grand scheme of things, it wouldn't make much of a difference, but for now, we'd won. Our little corner of the world was safer once again, even if just for now.

"Are you OK?" Penn said glancing at me for only a quick second before facing forward again. The further we got away from the burning buildings, the darker the path in front of us became.

"Yeah, I'm fine. Are you? It looked like he hit you pretty hard," I said remembering the physical battle between Penn and the man from HOME.

Penn chuckled. "Pretty sore, but I'll heal."

We didn't talk much for the rest of the walk. Penn was focused on getting us back to our place, and I couldn't get out of my head.

HOME would be back. They'd figure out what happened to their buildings and their men. Maybe they'd even go out looking for whoever was responsible, and since we didn't live far away, they'd probably get their revenge.

All we really did was delay the inevitable... again. But we had the tunnels. We wouldn't ever give up without a fight.

Several hours had probably passed by, but it hadn't felt that long when our house came into view. I couldn't have been happier to see it, and I was pretty sure Penn felt the same way.

I followed him to the garage where he left the gas can and then we walked back to the front of the house. Everything looked exactly the same as we had left it.

Penn's eyes scanned the ground, and I assumed he was looking for signs that someone had come around. I didn't see anything, and I thought since Penn didn't say anything, he hadn't either.

He opened the front door and gestured for me to go inside. Once we were both inside, he locked the door and stared out the window.

"You see something?" I asked as I took off my jacket.

Penn shook his head. "Just making sure."

I stood next to him, and he wrapped his arm around me. We'd been gone so long the sun was starting to peek out over the horizon. Even though my mind was racing, my body was tired. When I yawned, Penn hugged me tighter.

"Go on, get some rest," he said kissing the top of my head, moving his lips down until they met mine.

"You too?" I said noticing the orange glow to the sky in the distance. I could tell Penn was looking at it too.

He turned away, letting the curtain fall. "Sure."

"How long until they come looking?" I asked pressing my cheek against his chest. I could feel his heart beating inside.

"I'm not sure. But we'll be ready. I'll get back to work on the tunnels. Everything will be OK," Penn said tilting my chin, forcing me to look into his eyes.

I could tell he believed his words, but words couldn't save us when HOME came.

"They'll rebuild. Then they'll build even more."

"And we'll burn those all down too."

I swallowed hard and took a step back. "They'll find us."

"We'll fight. We'll hide. I'll do whatever it takes to keep you and everything we have here safe," Penn said with a warm smile. "I really believe it's going to be OK."

I smiled back and let out another yawn. My body relaxed for the first time in days, maybe even weeks. It would take time before HOME came, if they came… at this moment we were safe.

I took a step towards the bedroom trying to pull Penn along with me, but his feet were glued to the ground.

"Are you coming?" I asked cocking my head to the side.

"Go ahead. I'll be right there."

I could tell by the way his eyes were darting around the room that he just wanted to check everything out. He wanted to make sure everything was exactly in the right place.

I went into the bedroom and changed my clothes before lying down in the bed. The blankets were cool, but somehow the bed still felt warm, and comforting.

I let out a long sigh just as Penn walked into the room. He flopped down on the bed and sucked in a deep breath.

When I looked at him, I thought I was going to see stress and worry on his face, but I didn't. He was smiling.

Penn looked different. Relaxed. At peace. Happy… ish.

"Well this is new," I said closing my eyes as I cuddled up next to him.

"What?"

"You."

I felt his body tighten into a stretch and then relax. "Things are going to be different. I really have a good feeling. We are going to be OK."

There was something about the way he said it that made me actual believe it. Of course, we'd always be worried about HOME… that wasn't something that could, or should stop, but this time something just felt different.

We'd defended our little corner of the world, and it made it feel as though it belonged to us for real. We had claimed our land. And both Penn and I were committed to keeping it that way, and we would do anything to protect what was ours.

Penn had fallen asleep with what looked like a smile on his face. If he was content, then I knew I could be too.

Everything really was going to be all right. It took almost everything out of me to get here, but now that I was, I felt stronger. I felt as though I could do anything. And with Penn at my side, I was pretty sure I couldn't lose.

I'd somehow survived terrible struggles and tragedies. Things I never thought I'd be able to move past. Things that I thought might be the end of me. But here I was... still standing. I was more ready to fight for my life, and Penn's life, than ever before.

This world wasn't what any of us wanted, but this was how it was. All we had to do was make it the best we could. And that's what Penn and I were going to do. Whatever this world wanted to throw at us, we'd fight, and we'd survive.

Epilogue.

A few weeks after we burned down the HOME tower, I thought I'd gotten ill. I'd throw-up even when there wasn't anything in my belly, and I felt tired most of the time. Penn tried to hide his worry, but I could tell.

He'd place a cool cloth on my forehead and constantly pace. Asking every ten minutes if I needed anything.

There were times I thought I was feeling better, but then the next day, I'd wake up and feel sick all over again.

"This isn't anything like what the others went through," I said shaking my head. "It's been weeks, and most of the time I feel OK, but other times... bleck!"

"Hmm," Penn said as he tapped his chin with his fingertip. "You're right. But clearly something is making you ill."

I wrapped my arms around my middle as the strange taste filled my mouth. Penn looked at me as if my skin had actually turned green.

"If this were some kind of bug or something, you would have caught it by now," I said resting the back of my hand on my forehead.

"Right. And I feel fine." He reached over and lightly stroked my hair.

It was when he looked into my eyes I considered another possibility. Something that seemed pretty far-fetched, at least at first.

I placed my hand on my stomach and let out a breath between my lips. Was it possible? Hell, yes, it was possible. Penn and I had been together multiple times.

"What is it?" Penn asked noticing the look on my face.

Somehow, without any real knowledge on the subject, I realized what could be happening. It seemed crazy, but it was the only explanation I could think of that made sense. I was pregnant.

I wasn't sure what to say or how to even broach the subject. It wasn't like I could bring a baby into a world like this. Could I? Who would deliver it? What doctor would check to make sure the baby was OK?

"Dammit, Ros, you're making me nervous," Penn said twisting his fingers against one another. He scratched the back of his head, and it almost looked like he was going to be sick.

"OK. I had a thought, but this is probably crazy," I said taking a loud, awkward breath.

"Yes?"

"Um, OK, I don't know how to even say this exactly," I said as I stood up so I could pace.

Penn stepped in front of me and blocked my path. "You're just going to tell me so I can help you. We need to do whatever we can to get you well again."

I let out a puff of air. The idea of a baby wasn't even on his radar. I had no idea how he was going to take it. Even the thought of it could send him storming out of the house.

It wasn't even like I knew for sure. I was probably just being crazy.

"OK, don't freak out," I said watching as his eyes widened. I was pretty sure he was going to freak out. "This is going to sound bizarre, but I think there is a chance that maybe I could be…."

"Could be what, Ros?"

"OK, um, here goes," I said placing my palms outward as though I was making an offering, "pregnant."

He stared at my hands with his nose scrunched up for at least a minute before shifting his eyes upwards. I could tell he was trying to determine if I was serious or not.

"Really? Is that even possible? I mean I know, obviously, it's possible, but... really?" he said with his eyebrows pinched together tightly.

I shrugged and clenched my teeth together into a strange smile I'd never worn before. "I don't know for sure of course, it was just a thought really, but—"

"Let's find out for sure," Penn said disappearing from the room. His feet pounded against the stairs as he ran down to the basement. Within thirty seconds he was back up pushing a box into my hand. "Here."

"Why on earth do we have these?" I asked with a raised eyebrow.

Penn shook his head vigorously. "Carter grabbed them on his first run. I told him to take anything and everything. And that's exactly what he did. I remember laughing with him when we shelved them. I don't think he even realized what he'd taken. Who knew it would ever come in handy?"

"Maybe. It's expired. Might not give accurate results."

"Let's find out." Penn smiled and gestured towards the bathroom. I was surprised he wasn't freaking out more. In fact, I was surprised I wasn't freaking out more.

I closed myself in the bathroom and locked the door. Once I was alone, all the reasons this couldn't happen flooded my mind. How could we bring a child into this world? With HOME out there wanting to get rid of us.

It took me a solid five minutes to build up the courage to pee on the stick, even though I was pretty sure I already knew what I would find once the time was up. I covered my eyes and counted. When it was time, I pulled my hands down slowly and stared at the positive pregnancy test sitting on the edge of the sink.

My mind went blank. I didn't know what to say or think or feel, and I was worried what Penn was going to say, think and feel.

"Everything OK in there?" He asked

as he lightly knocked on the door.

"Yeah, fine."

"Can I come in yet?"

I left the stick on the edge of the sink and unlocked the door. After a few seconds, Penn turned the knob.

He didn't have to look at the stick to know what it said. Everything about me must have revealed the results.

"Wow. Um. OK," he said taking in a deep breath. After a few seconds, he looked down at the stick as though he wanted visual proof. "Wow."

"Yeah," I said swallowing hard. I didn't know what to say because the news hadn't really sunk in for me either.

"We're going to have a baby?"

Suddenly a smile appeared on his face, and with each passing second, it got bigger. He picked me up and kissed me before spinning me in a circle in the small bathroom.

"We're going to have a baby!" he said in a voice filled with joy.

I nodded, my smile unexpectedly matching his. I'd never seen Penn so happy.

"This is the greatest news! I mean I wish it was under better circumstances, but damn, this is amazing. I can't wait to meet him… to teach him everything I know," Penn put his hand on my stomach.

"Who said anything about it being a him?" I said with a half-smile.

"It doesn't matter. She'll be one tough, little, kick-ass girl."

Over the next several months we took turns alternating being excited with being scared. Almost all of the time we were both happy with the little bundle that would soon change our lives even more than they already had been.

This child would grow up in this world not ever knowing what had been. He or she wouldn't know there had been televisions, phones or computers. Everything we would tell him, or her, would sound like a fairytale.

Penn had taken two runs during those nine months. He hadn't wanted to leave me alone for long, but he insisted on getting diapers, baby food, and anything else he could find in the baby aisles we might need.

I wasn't even the least bit surprised when he came back with books about how to take care of a baby. But I was surprised when he took the time to read them.

When it came time to actually have the baby, Penn stepped up. He did something so amazing… he delivered our baby.

We both laughed and cried when that tiny little being that we created let out its loud cry. The one that would tell HOME exactly where we were, but we didn't care about that. The only thing we cared about was that little baby.

"What should we name her?" Penn said putting his arm around me, both of us gazing down at the little one snuggled in my arm.

We hadn't allowed ourselves to talk about names, just in case, but now that she was here, we needed one. I looked down at her cute, content little face. She didn't give a crap about the world she was born into. She just wanted a safe, warm place to snuggle.

"I don't know," I said unable to take my eyes off of her for more than a second. If it wasn't for the soreness, I could have convinced myself it had all been a dream.

She was just so perfect. But she didn't know what kind of world she'd entered. She'd have to be brave, have courage, and be strong. The little girl in my arms wouldn't have a choice in the matter, she would have to be a fighter.

"What do you think of Emery?" I asked taking my eyes off of her for only a split second. The smile the spread across his face told me he was on board.

"Hello, little Emery. Welcome to our family," Penn said lightly stroking her cheek with his thumb as he kissed me on the top of my head. "How did I get so lucky?"

I wanted to argue, but I couldn't. At that moment, even after everything, I felt it too. I was… happy.

As the months passed, Emery grew like a weed. Penn worked on his tunnels any chance he got, but most of the time he spent staring at our daughter with little hearts in his eyes.

He told me all the time how much he loved Emery and me. Constantly reminding us how much we meant to him and how he'd do anything for us.

We both knew that one day, we'd have to explain the world outside our doors to her. That one day she might have to face HOME with us. Penn would teach her everything he knew, and she'd be strong. She'd fight.

One day HOME would come, but we'd be ready. We'd stay and fight, or if that didn't work, we'd have the tunnels.

We'd figure it out.

We'd make it work.

We had survived, and we would continue to survive.

The End.

Books By Kellee L. Greene

Ravaged Land Series
Ravaged Land -Book 1
Finding Home - Book 2
Crashing Down - Book 3
Running Away - Book 4
Escaping Fear - Book 5
Fighting Back - Book 6

The Alien Invasion Series
The Landing - Book 1
The Aftermath - Book 2

Destined Realms
Destined - Book 1

About the Author

Kellee L. Greene is a stay-at-home-mom to two super awesome and wonderfully sassy children. She loves to read, draw and spend time with her family when she's not writing. Writing and having people read her books has been a long time dream of hers and she's excited to write more. Her favorites genres are Fantasy and Sci-fi. Kellee lives in Wisconsin with her husband, two kids and two cats.

Coming Soon

Kellee is currently working on several new projects, including another series. Please follow Kellee L. Greene on Facebook to be one of the first to hear about what's new.

www.facebook.com/kelleelgreene

Mailing List

Sign up for Kellee L. Greene's newsletter for new releases, sales, cover reveals and more!

http://eepurl.com/bJLmrL

Dear Reader,

Wow. What a ride. I can't believe it's over! Thank you so much for taking this journey with me. Writing Ravaged Land was a dream come true and putting those last words down have been very bittersweet.

Thanks to everyone who ever shared my books, or told others about them. It's people like you that make writers' dreams a reality. I cannot thank you enough.

To all of those who stayed up late just to read one more chapter - I hope I can bring you that again in another series and in the meantime, rest up.

A super special thanks to my husband who puts up with me working most nights and weekends. And of course listening to me talk about my ideas nearly all the time. You helped make this possible.

To my kids, make your dreams come true. Do what you love, do it a lot, and hopefully the rest will fall into place.

Thanks to Kelly D. For all that word of mouth advertising!

Friends… family… everyone who read my books… THANK YOU!

In 2013 I lost my mom to cancer. I really wish she could have been here to see what I accomplished.

In 2016 I lost my dad. He missed her terribly. Both gone way too soon.

I love and miss them both so much.

To everyone with dreams, start today. You can make them your reality. Take that first step and get started today.

Hope you all join me again soon on the next journey.

Until then,

Kellee L. Greene